RISA NYMAN

SWALLOWED BY A SECRET

Appropriate for Teens, Intriguing to Adults

Immortal Works LLC
1505 Glenrose Drive
Salt Lake City, Utah 84104
Tel: (385) 202-0116

Cover Art by Ashley Literski
http://strangedevotion.wixsite.com/strangedesigns

This book is a work of fiction. Names, characters, businesses, organizations, places, events and incidents either are the product of the author's imagination or are used fictitiously. Any resemblance to actual persons, living or dead, events, or locales is entirely coincidental.

ISBN 978-1-7343866-1-5 (Paperback)
ASIN B082XGMT39 (Kindle Edition)

For Philip, who always stands beside me and makes everything possible

CHAPTER 1

I glance at my yellow schedule card, already moist from first-day palm sweat, and trudge up the stairs to my third-floor homeroom. This is officially the second-worst day of my life.

I shouldn't have to be here today. I belong in my old school with my friends. Why Mom couldn't see that is something I'll never understand.

The teacher's desk is at the back of the room. I make my way there. For the longest time, she doesn't notice me. *Hey, look up, teacher, new kid here.* I give up and subtly wave my yellow card in her face. It works. She looks up with eyelids stuck between awake and asleep—and it's only 8:05 in the morning—and checks me off her list.

"Welcome to Tucker Middle, Ronald."

Ronald. Ugh. Changing schools is a nightmare. You have to

create your life all over again. You have to explain everything, including not to call me Ronald.

I guess no one here at Tucker will know my name has been Rocky since the first grade when I complained to my dad about being Ronald Owen Casson, Jr. and not having my own name. He made up the nickname Rocky for me by using my initials R.O.C. and ever since that's who I am.

But today, I'm not correcting anyone. My plan is to fly under the radar and try to blend in. I don't need any attention on me.

The teacher hands me a piece of paper with a name and room number and says, "You're scheduled to meet with the school counselor after homeroom."

"Already?" I ask, shocked they can't even wait a week before they haul me in for "the talk." The counselor probably reviewed my recent less-than-stellar record, but despite what Mom may think, I'm not on a slippery slope to repeating seventh grade. It was only a temporary lapse and a few too many "sick" days after Dad died. Mom shouldn't give up on me yet.

"Yes, today," the teacher says. "Take a seat." She points to a desk in the last row near the windows.

I stuff my backpack under the desk and look around. The room is noisy with loud laughing coming from a group of boys in the corner. Two of them are shoving each other but not hard enough to catch the teacher's tired eyes. The girls next to me are yakking non-stop and from time-to-time looking in my direction. I'm sure they're talking about me—the new flavor in Tucker Middle.

The teacher begins the morning announcements about a spirit rally and school dance, which float through my ears like meaningless vapor. Then she makes me stand up and introduces me to the class. I cringe from the friggin' attention and stuff my hands into my pockets to hide their twitching. All eyes examine the alien who dropped into their midst.

Being the new kid sucks big time, and it's way worse when you change schools in the middle of the year. Mom couldn't even wait until summer as if some big emergency was forcing us to get out of Whitman without delay. She made us move in March. The "For Sale" sign was stuck in the front lawn right after the funeral.

I asked her if we had to move because of a money thing.

"No," she said.

"Are we moving in with Grandpa because he's sick?"

"No."

I argued. I pleaded. I cried. I lost.

The end-of-homeroom bell jolts that awful memory out of my brain. I join the hordes going to the first floor and plaster on a smile in preparation for my meeting with the counselor so she'll know I'm okay, and doesn't put me on permanent appointment status.

I walk up and down the hallway but can't find the counselor's office. I'm getting suspicious that the school hid her office so the "troubled" kids wouldn't be seen going in and out. Luckily, I spot a guy nearby mopping up a puddle of gunk.

As I approach, the usual odor of school disinfectant slams into my nostrils. The Tucker custodian must buy his foul-smelling potions to clean whatever horrors are inflicted on the walls and floors of the school from the same catalog as the Whitman guy. I ask him where Ms. Malone's office is. He lifts up his mop and aims the handle at a door diagonally across the hall.

I knock. A short, pudgy woman with mostly gray hair pulled tight into a bunch sitting on the top of her head opens the door and sticks out her hand, so I do too. She pumps it as if she expects to fill a bucket with my blood. Ms. Malone's dark eyes remind me of Shawny's grandma's even though Ms. Malone's skin isn't as dark.

"I thought you might've gotten lost. Are you having difficulty finding your way around the school?"

"No." I use my specialty—one-word answers. This is a technique I perfected when people said dumb stuff like "Your dad was a great guy, but I'm sure you know that" or "Now you'll have to take care of your mother and be the man of the house." Did people really imagine a twelve-year-old is going to be in charge of anything? I'd answer,

"Yeah," and clam up until extreme awkwardness filled the quiet space, and they'd move on to try their luck elsewhere.

I'm not into sharing what's on my mind. When Mom asked if I wanted to say something at Dad's funeral, my answer was a firm, loud "no."

Ms. Malone doesn't seem bothered by my short response. She continues, "Rocky, I'm delighted to meet you today. I want you to be comfortable coming here any time, for any reason." She smiles at me, all cheery, as if the mere sight of me makes her supremely happy.

"Okay," I reply, grateful that at least she knows my *real* name.

"I'm sorry for your loss, Rocky," she says, not hesitating to dive right into the main subject. "Losing a parent is always difficult, but when it's so sudden, it must be harder."

"Yeah," I say. What else can a person say? Difficult, oh sure.

"And he was so young," Ms. Malone says.

Sudden. Young. Maybe she's suspicious too like I was when Mom told me the "his heart just stopped" story. On the morning of the funeral, I looked for Mom to ask if my tie was okay and overheard Shawny's mom telling Mom she was in control of what to tell me and when. Ms. R. said, "Marybeth, no regrets. People die from heart problems all the time. It's a totally believable story."

From then on, I've been convinced Mom's covering up something; maybe it's a secret too horrible for a kid to know. Most likely, she is overdoing the overprotecting. Either way, she has tossed trust in the garbage. This secret is keeping Mom and me separated as if a massive elephant has plunked itself down between us and refuses to move.

Ms. Malone must have noticed my brain was roaming, because she asks, "Are you okay, Rocky?"

"Young," I repeat. Even if I wanted to say more, I've nothing to add and lower my eyes, rubbing the tops of my thighs to smooth out imaginary wrinkles in my jeans.

Ms. Malone clears her throat. "Will you come see me if you have any problems?"

I doubt she means helping me find out the truth. All my other counselors stuck with Mom's story. Maybe that's all they knew too. Dad dies, Mom makes us move, and poof, my whole life changes. Maybe I could enlist Ms. Malone to persuade Mom to at least let me go back to Whitman for the summer soccer clinic.

I lift my head up, and there's a meltiness in Ms. Malone's face that makes her eyes and mouth go all soft. She probably got an A++ in the kindness course in counselor school. She's different than the last guy I saw who bored me with endless descriptions of a beach in Saint something where he was going on his upcoming vacation.

Ms. Malone slips on her glasses, which were hanging around her neck, and reads one of the papers in my folder. I wish I had Superman vision and could bore my eyes into that file. I bet there's stuff written in the folder I should know. I stretch my neck until it almost snaps off in an attempt to read upside down. It doesn't work.

"Rocky, we hope your schoolwork will improve here, and you'll be on track for success. A good start is important, don't you agree?"

"Yeah." Now she's gonna think I have the vocabulary of a three-year-old.

Ms. Malone replaces the paper, closes the folder and stands—the universal sign the meeting has ended. "Everyone at Tucker is ready to help you."

She asks if I need directions to Social Studies. I shake my head and scoot out.

In the hallway, I remove my smile, happy that went—

WELL.

THAT VOICE. I never thought I'd hear it again. My eyes dart in all directions. I pivot 180 degrees to check behind me. What do I expect to see? Ice slides down my spine and into my legs, which are frozen.

Dead people don't talk.

CHAPTER 2

I stare down at my feet, trying to melt the ice with my piercing eyes. It works, and I dash for the nearest restroom, which fortunately is empty. I run into a stall and pull the door closed. I press my palm deep into my chest to slow the NASCAR laps my heart's doing. This stress can't be good for my health.

YOU SHOULDN'T BE SCARED OF YOUR OWN FATHER, the voice says.

My hands can't stop shaking, so I stuff them into my pockets to calm them down. I don't actually believe in ghosts. They're okay for Halloween and the movies, but not in real life.

I'M NOT A GHOST, the voice says.

He "heard" what I was thinking. How is that possible? My dead father is inside my head. He sounds like he always did and not dead, but how the heck would I know how a dead person is supposed to sound? Maybe this is a hallucination caused by the most severe case of new-school jitters ever. This never happened to me in Whitman.

You are not hallucinating, Dad says, and I didn't talk to you in Whitman because you didn't need me there. I want to help you. You're my number one son.

That was Dad's all-time favorite cornball line. Whenever, he said it, he wanted me to respond with "and you're my number one father," but I never did. I thought it sounded silly—and now it's too late for that.

I open the door to the stall very, very slowly, not sure what might be lurking there. I take baby steps to the mirror, hoping my wobbly legs don't cave and land me on the disgusting bathroom floor. What if I see my dead father standing beside me? The mirror is worn and mostly blurry, but I find a clear spot. Dad isn't in the reflection, only me with enormous, frightened saucers for eyes as if I've seen a ghost, but I haven't really.

I'm not a ghost, Dad repeats. I want to help you uncover the truth.

Perhaps I've been transported to a parallel universe where dead people talk. This is way too sci-fi for me. My imagination is running wild.

You have to find a way to get to Whitman. That's where the answers are. Dad's voice is urgent and insistent.

My real dad would know that's impossible. Mom has put Whitman in the no-go column.

We'll find a way, Dad says.

"Why don't you tell me the truth? If anyone knows what really happened to you, it should be you." I can't believe I am talking to my dead father. This can't be normal.

I can't tell you what happened. You have to go back to Whitman, Dad says.

Doesn't he get how crazy that idea is?

It's not crazy. Trust me. Again, he answers a question I haven't asked him.

Trust him? How is that supposed to work? He's dead.

A slow, rolling stream emerges from my eyes, which I try to keep in check with the sleeve of my hoodie, but the water keeps coming. I want to ditch school, but I can't risk it. Mom will assume I'm sliding into my old bad habits.

Do not ditch school. Mom will be upset, Dad says.

"Can you at least please, please not talk to me in school? I've already got a lot to deal with today." I'm negotiating with a voice in my head. This weirdness has gone stratospheric.

I won't. Word of honor, he promises.

I'm not sure if dead people follow the same rules as everyone else when it comes to sticking to their word of honor. I guess I'll find out.

I leave the restroom and go to Social Studies. The teacher spots me as soon as I enter the classroom and zips over to greet me. I give him my late pass from Ms. Malone.

"Hello, I'm Mr. Handler. Welcome to Tucker." He shakes my hand like I'm a grown-up and directs me to a seat in the back near the windows. Clearly, this is the official Tucker Middle School location for newbies in case we decide to throw ourselves out the window. Ha. Ha.

Kids huddle in groups working on something. Mr. Handler heads my way, leaning into me with his coffee breath. "What unit were you working on in your old school?"

I've been mostly a zombie in school since Dad died, I'm drawing blanks on his question. Finally, I confess, "Er...I don't remember."

"But you completed the map of the world project, didn't you? I think it's standard curriculum in the county."

"Um...maybe." I have no idea.

"Let's check that out. Follow me," he says.

He leads me to a large globe on a wooden stand wedged in a corner and informs me he's partial to globes because they give a different perspective than maps on a flat screen. He spins the large ball and lets it slow to a stop.

"Can you point out Germany?" he asks.

I have no choice but to guess and pick a country in a nice light green color on the opposite side of the United States. Mr. Handler looks gut-punched. I must be way off.

"Let's try another place. Can you find Chile? I'll give you a hint. It has an unusual shape."

This is more of a problem, but I take a stab at it. Mr. Handler's hand rushes up to cover his mouth, but not fast enough. A small smile peeks out.

"Hmmm. That's not quite right," he says. "No problem, Rocky. I'll assign you a geography partner so you can catch up. This information is a basis for the explorers' unit we're working on."

Partners. Ugh! No one wants to be partners with a new kid, but I nod in agreement. What I want to explain to him is geography is super useless in this age when everyone has a GPS on their cell. If anyone types an address into their phone, the satellites do the rest.

"Olivia, could you come here for a minute?" Mr. Handler asks.

A very tall, and I mean a tower of a girl, walks over. I'm average size, but next to her, I feel shrimpy.

"Olivia is our geography star. You two should set up a time to meet and review that unit."

Mr. Handler leaves us and goes off to bother some other kids. My nervous feet shift as if they're preparing to dance right here, right now. Not sure what I'm supposed to say. Fortunately, she speaks first.

"What's your name?" she asks.

"Roc—"

Before I get the "ky" out, she interrupts, "Rock, like a piece of granite?"

"No. Roc like in Rocky."

"Never met a Rocky before."

I'm sure she has no idea that the real Rocky was an undefeated, heavyweight champion from Massachusetts who lived decades ago.

Most people only think about the prizefighter in the movie *Rocky* who's famous for running up a million steps at a museum in Philadelphia. Sometimes I stand in front of the mirror and pretend I'm in the ring, dancing around and practicing my jabs and left crosses.

"You should call me Olive. Do you eat olives?"

"No." I'm not sharing with her that I avoid all dreaded green foods. No exceptions.

"Me either, which is wrong, considering it's my name. And for your information, cross country, not basketball."

"Huh?"

"You would eventually ask me if I'm the female Michael Jordan; now you don't have to. No hoops. I run. So, delete that question from your list."

"What list?" My brain cells are doing the dog paddle, while hers are training for the 100-meter freestyle.

"The list of things we have to know about each other." She grabs my hand and writes her phone number on my palm. "Text me later and we'll make plans to work on this at my house."

"Huh?" This conversation is moving too fast for me. I'm racing to keep up with it, but I think I'm failing.

"You do have a phone, don't you?"

"Yeah," I respond, wondering why the dummy in me is trying to show off to this girl.

When the bell rings, she asks, "Are you smart?" She's probably convinced I have a serious shortage of brain matter.

"Um...yeah," I say.

She gives me a smirky look as if she doubts my answer and then disappears into a mob of kids in the hallway.

So now, I guess I'm going to a girl's house for the first time when it isn't her birthday party or a whole class thing. This isn't supposed to be a biggie in middle school, but it might be for me.

CHAPTER 3

C ould this day get any more complicated?

By the time I get to the cafeteria for first lunch period, my stomach is on a raft floating on an angry sea. Anything I eat might resurface quickly. I grab a tray and spot the familiar rubbery chicken nuggets and wilted French fries they serve at Whitman Middle on Mondays. On any other day, this could be a comforting reminder of home, but today, this junk food assaults my already nervous digestive system.

I survey the scene and head for a table far away from the middle of the room, which is usually the territory of the popular kids so they can see everyone, and everyone can see them. A newcomer and a don't-belonger should stay away from ground zero of the popular zone.

I pick a table where a boy is sitting alone. I put down my tray.

He stares up at me and spits out, "Get lost, Fartwad. No one invited you here."

"But—" I stammer.

The jerk stands. He's a hulk. I'm not messing with him. I pick up my tray and find an empty table. A few seconds later, Olive shows up and sits down.

As she unpacks her sandwich, yogurt and chips, she eyeballs me in a way that sends squirm signals to my butt.

"So, Rocky, where are you from?" she asks.

"Whitman."

"Where's that?"

"About an hour from here."

"Why did you move now? Your parents change jobs? You get into trouble?" Her eyebrows rise into question marks waiting for my response.

The way she looks at me makes me super self-conscious.

I have no answer even if I wanted to tell her. I'm sure there's a connection between Dad's dying and Mom's wanting to escape from Whitman, but I don't know what it is. Mom's afraid of something in our old town, but when I ask her what's really going on, it's like riding on a Ferris Wheel. I go around and around with her and always end where I began.

I keep my mouth full so I don't have to answer Olive's question. She gets the hint and moves on to a new topic, describing all the cliques at Tucker Middle and which tables to stay clear of at all times.

When lunch ends, Olive says, "You need an experienced Tuckerite to guide you. That will be me," pointing at herself. "Rocket Man, come over tomorrow for geography lessons."

"Can't. Soccer practice."

"So, the day after."

"I'll ask."

We split for our next classes, and I feel like a wind cyclone just expelled me from its grasp. Olive is a force of nature, whirling around me. Zoning out in her presence could be perilous.

The next classes go on forever as I fixate on the giant clocks above the teachers' desks and watch their hands move slower than a senior citizen snail. It takes forever for it to get to 3:00.

When the final bell rings, I bolt, slowing, only to dodge patches of icy, dirty snow. All the while I repeat the directions from Tucker to Grandpa's house Mom drilled into me, so she'd at least know one thing today: no way I'm getting lost.

When I reach the front door, my hand automatically reaches into my pocket for the key until I remember I don't have one because it's not my house. I press the button, and the chimes play their tune, bringing Grandpa to the door.

"Hi, Grandpa. I'm going up to work on homework. I'm behind in everything." This is an excuse, because I have to be alone and figure out what the heck is going on with me today.

Grandpa says, "Okay." He returns to the den and his reading chair without asking any questions about my day. He is not at all the talkative type. At Dad's funeral, he patted my head a few times and said, "There's nothing much to say." He was right, but still.

As soon as I'm in my room, not my room, just the room I sleep in now, I ask, "Dad, are you here?"

CHAPTER 4

There must be something the matter with me if I'm actually talking to my dead father. Maybe this is some sort of a funky mind trick. But to be on the safe side, I retrieve my bat and crouch down to check under the bed. Shoving my soccer bag to one side, I wave the bat around in case an invisible being is hiding under there. But wouldn't a bat pass through a ghost's body? They don't have actual bodies, do they?

I TOLD YOU I'M NOT A GHOST, Dad says.

Oh no! The voice is back.

I examine the closet. No sign of him in there. I climb on the bed, gather my knees to my chest and hold them tight to control the shakes, and wait. It's quiet for a while, so limb-by-limb, I unwind my body and uncurl my muscles.

Buddy, first days are rough, Dad says.

I'm beyond freaked.

"You're scaring me," I say into the air. "What are you?"

I'm Dad, and I want to help you uncover the real story so you'll know what happened to me.

"I can't understand why you can't tell me the truth."

I just can't.

He obviously isn't the all-knowing kind of spirit.

I'm not a ghost, and I'm not a spirit. Go back to Whitman for the answers you need.

Yeah, right. Everyone knows you have to return to the scene of a crime. Is that what this is? A crime? My real dad would realize I have no way to get there on my own.

"Should I take a taxi there?" I ask with a smart aleck mouth, but does it count as being rude if the person you're talking to is dead?

Too much money, he jokes.

I laugh. His great sense of humor is still there. I inherited that from him, at least I hope I did. "Hey, Dad, if you want to do something for me, figure out a way to get Mom to let me go to summer soccer in Whitman."

Before Dad died, he and I were pumped that I'd be able to train with a pro goalie this summer. He said it would be great prep so I could play varsity when I'm in high school.

But now, I don't hear him offering me any help to go to the soccer clinic. I threaten him. "I'm gonna tell Mom you're talking to me."

You can if you want, Dad says, but she might have a stroke.

Heck, I might be the one to have a stroke.

I reach for my laptop and Google "dead people talking." The first hit is for a movie, *The Dead Talk the Talk*. It's a fantasy horror flick and rated R, so I won't be allowed to see it.

The next hit takes me to a page describing a medium claiming to communicate with the dead. I click on that link. A woman in California believes she can talk with murder victims and have them identify their killers. Most detectives consider her a phony. I agree. If she could do what she claims, no innocent people would ever be locked up. More likely, she's running a giant hoax to con money from believers.

Google has nothing about hearing the voice of a dead relative. I'm about to change my search criteria when the door opens. Mom marches in without knocking, which is in direct violation of the pact we agreed to when I turned twelve. I'm supposed to be entitled to some privacy, but I'm not getting any today.

I close the computer fast because Mom has privileges to check my online stuff whenever she wants. I think she can do that until I'm in high school. She slumps on the desk chair, kicks off her shoes, and wheels it closer to the bed. Whew. At least, this isn't a "check his computer" day.

"I came home early to find out how your first day was. Why are you in bed?" she asks.

"Um...no reason...just doing homework on the computer." *Quick save*, I tell myself.

Mom studies me with familiar blue eyes. They're the same eyes I see when I look in the mirror. I may have Dad's name, but I've got her eyes and blond hair, which I don't mind. I'm just grateful I didn't inherit her dimple.

Mom examines the room and says, "Sorry about the colors in here. My old room doesn't suit you. We'll have to redecorate."

I'll have to live with hideous light pink walls and lacey white curtains. Even the quilt is an abomination of oversized purple and bright pink flowers. When I pull it all the way over me, it's like I'm being buried in an ugly garden.

I blame her for the room and for everything. "Well, my old room, in my old house, on my old street, in my old town was perfect." I'm sure the snark comes through loud and clear.

"You're upset about the move. I understand," she says, "I can't ask Grandpa for extra money to repaint now. You'll have to live in this pink room a little while longer."

"Whatever," I say, invoking the perfect word for out-of-touch parents. "Is our house sold already?"

"Not yet."

My questions bring on a familiar sadness in her voice, but all this is her fault and not mine. She's the one who made us move.

"Is there even a sliver of a chance we could go back home?"

"No. I'm sorry."

"Why would you want to leave all the stuff that reminds us of Dad?" I miss the rainbow wall we painted in the basement, the place in the backyard where grass never grows because of all the soccer practice and the climbing tree whose trunk divides into a "V," where Dad and I would perch to survey the neighborhood. All that is gone now.

"That's not what this is about."

Whatever she's hiding is staying hidden. I'm gonna have to crack open her secrets by myself.

CUT HER SOME SLACK, Dad's voice says to me right in front of Mom.

I check Mom's face for a reaction, but there's no change. I guess no one else can hear him. I freeze my mouth and bite the inside of my cheek so I don't let on that anything out of the ordinary is happening. If Mom knew this, she might move us even farther away for a bigger real "fresh start," maybe as far as Timbuktu, which is supposed to be the farthest place from here. I should ask Olive where that is. She's the geography-lover.

"How was your day?" Mom asks, "Meet any new kids?"

Most parents believe friends are the cure if you're upset. It's not always true, but when you hang with your friends, it kinda lets them off the hook.

"Not really," I say.

"You'll make friends soon." She's clueless to think I can trade in Shawny for a newer best-friend model like buying a car.

"I had plenty of friends in Whitman." She's got to be reminded what she's done to me.

Dad butts in, TELL HER ABOUT THE GIRL WHO SAT WITH YOU AT LUNCH AND EYED YOU IN THAT I-LIKE-YOU WAY GIRLS HAVE WHEN THEY'RE SENDING A BOY A MESSAGE.

He's out of his gourd if he thinks I'm doing that.

Mom repeats, "You'll have friends. You're a great kid. Give it time. Dinner at six," and she's off.

As soon as she's gone, Dad says, WE'LL HAVE TO FIGURE OUT A WAY TO GET YOU TO WHITMAN. IT WILL BE OUR SPECIAL PROJECT.

Oh, no! Do NOT make me one of your projects. Dad's projects were legendary, but not in a good way. He'd always begin them with wild enthusiasm and most often they'd end in disaster.

Last year, he decided to build a deck on the house. And before a single nail went in, Dad was back at Home Hardware to buy a ready-to-make shed for the wood and tools in case it rained. He returned with not only the shed, but also a ladder to clean the gutters and paint for the front fence. He worked for days on all the projects at once in a frenzy until exhaustion overtook him. Then, suddenly he was off on another of his business trips. While he was away, Mom hired a handyman to finish the deck and the ready-to-assemble shed, clean the gutters and paint the fence. And I never got my assistant's pay Dad had promised me.

Later during dinner, Mom reminds me that I have soccer practice tomorrow at 6:00. I guess I do have enough time for a review session with Olive before that.

"Mom, I was assigned a partner in Social Studies to review geography. The kid wants me to come over to study. Can I go before practice?"

"What's his name?"

"Olive," I answer, keeping it cool.

"A girl." The corners of Mom's mouth shift into the beginnings of a full-blown, teeth-showing smile. "Do you know where she lives?"

"No. We'll go from school, and she can walk me home. She's lived here forever." I may be exaggerating, but she does seem to have the intel on everyone at Tucker.

"Will there be an adult at her house?" Mom is strict about that rule.

"I'll ask."

"And be home by 5:00 to get ready for soccer."

"Okay."

"And have fun."

There's a gleam in her eyes that gives me an icky feeling. I only just met Olive, and she is NOT my friend. We got stuck together so I could learn where Chile is.

CHAPTER 5

Back in my room, I check the number on my palm and text Olive.

Me: I can come tomorrow.

My phone pings back in an instant. Her cell must be velcroed to her hand.

Olive: excellent.

Me: will your PU be home?

Olive sends a thumbs up emoji and texts: mom. meet after school by green doors.

That's settled.

Before bed, I survey the room once more, leave the door cracked open and put the bedside light on dim. Then, to drown out any unwanted voices during the night, I put in my ear buds and set up a Hip Hop and Rap playlist on a loop.

I struggle to keep my eyes open and stay alert, but gradually drift off. Images of Mom on the phone listening to Uncle Bob explain that Dad was in the hospital appear behind my eyelids. Dad had been too tired to come with us to Florida for her boss's son's wedding and made plans to hang at home with his brother that weekend. The last time I saw Dad was when he waved as we went through security at the airport and called out that he loves us.

Our trip from Florida took forever, and when we landed at Logan Airport, we went straight to the hospital, but it was too late. Uncle Bob explained he had gone out to pick up some take-out and got a flat tire. He was gone for maybe three hours. When he got to our house, Dad was in a bad way. He called 911 immediately.

Uncle Bob held Mom as a raging river behind her eyes made tears gush like a geyser. It was all unbelievable. I had questions, but Uncle Bob kept his focus on Mom, patting her back and whispering in her ear. The next few days and weeks were a whirlwind with a blur of people always around.

WHEN MY ALARM rings at 6:30 A.M. the next morning, I sit upright, relieved the night passed without a peep from Dad's voice. I chalk up what happened yesterday to nervousness and decide this is a good omen for day two at Tucker. I hike up the blinds and open the window to breathe in the cool, clean smell.

I brush my teeth extra hard and comb my hair in a losing attempt to keep it off my forehead. I dislike hair products ever since another of Dad's over-the-top experiments. He had gathered a box overflowing with tubes, spray cans and jars of hair products. He bragged it took him a month to collect them from more than twenty stores. He made me test each one. I hated the stickiness. As the stuff hardened on my hair, I'd dunk my head under the kitchen faucet and wash it out.

By the time I got to the last tube, I used the thick goo to plaster down my hair so it looked painted on. Dad thought it was funny, but Mom was annoyed. Nothing was ever simple with Dad.

No goop today, but I do put on extra deodorant. If you smell, you can get labeled, and once you're labeled in middle school, it sticks to you like super glue.

I head downstairs. Mom already left, so Grandpa gives me breakfast. I can't find anything around here except the milk, which is obviously kept in the refrigerator. Big whoop for that.

I eat, grab my backpack and call out, "Bye, Grandpa."

He mumbles, "Goor-umph," which might be his version of goodbye or good luck.

As I get closer to the school, the sidewalk fills with noisy kids. Some are still digesting breakfast like me, and others are praying there won't be any pop quizzes like me. The rest could be counting the hours until 3:00, also like me.

I shift my backpack to the other shoulder, push open Tucker's heavy door and hope the not-a-ghost's voice will be absent from school today.

Morning classes pass without any unwanted interruptions. By the time I make my way to the cafeteria, I'm more relaxed. I choose the same empty table as yesterday. Studying the food in front of me, I try to guess what whacky ingredients they've put in today.

Man-up and make your own lunch, buddy, Dad says, responding to my inner griping.

The voice. Again. Startled, I jump up and bang into that fool who gave me a hard time yesterday.

"What's with you, Fartarolla?" the jerk asks.

Dad says, Tell him to buzz off.

"No," I answer, aware I have forgotten to keep my words inside.

"No, what?" the caveman asks, assuming my no was for him. "Don't be messing with me."

"Uh...," I mutter, trying to figure out my next move, when Olive shows up.

She says, "Move on, Max. Don't be such a donkey."

Max sticks his face into mine. "Lucky you've got a girl protecting you." And off he goes.

Olive and I sit down. I do the stress-relieving breathing a counselor in Whitman taught me for these types of situations.

Olive says, "You should avoid Max. He's like the plague around here." She gives me the low down on the giant, who came to Milton in fifth grade and has zero friends which is no surprise, given his "winning" personality.

CHAPTER 6

Olive's already waiting for me at 3:00, doing the wall-lean. She has an end-of-the-school-day look with two hunks of hair that ejected from the elastic holder hanging loosely by her face. Most seventh-grade girls constantly check their hair, add more lip-gloss or use a special skinny pencil to draw lines around their eyes. Olive doesn't care about stuff like that. She wears no make-up. I assume she hates products as much as I do.

She lives pretty close to the school. Before Olive even turns her key, her mom opens the door. She's wearing jeans and a t-shirt with a prowling tiger. This is such a different look than my mom who has to wear business suits to work. Mom complains there's nothing more boring than accountants and their clothes. She doesn't even get casual Fridays.

After the intros, Olive's mom leads us into the kitchen where an enormous platter of strawberries, cheese sticks and snickerdoodles and two glasses of chocolate milk welcomes us. I'm curious if Olive gets these after school treats every day, or if this display of kid-favorite foods is because of me.

Her mom asks how I'm liking Milton.

I lie and say, "So far, so good."

When we finish eating, I follow Olive into what she calls "the family room." She explains she isn't allowed to have boys in her room as though apologizing for that. Kids always hung out in my room, but then again, none of them were girls. There might be some new rules about this, but no one told me. I sit on the sofa, and Olive sprawls on the floor and starts spreading out papers with blank maps.

Olive and I review geography stuff, and then she says, "Enough for today. Don't want to clutter your head too much. Now no more dodging yesterday's question. Why DID you move in the middle of the school year? Spill already."

"I don't want my life's story broadcast all over school."

"I do not have diarrhea mouth."

I know you have to be careful, because middle schools churn out gossip faster than Muhammad Ali's knockout of Sonny Liston for the heavyweight title. Rumors in Whitman could be harsh. Once a kid told a girl he liked her, and he was doomed. By the end of the day, the whole sixth grade had the news. His face stayed red for weeks until someone else assumed the title of Star of a New Gossip Story.

"How can I be sure you won't tell?" I ask, shifting from one butt cheek to the other, which produces suspicious noisy cracks on the leather sofa. Olive's gonna think I'm gross, but she doesn't scrunch up her nose or anything, so I'm guessing this probably isn't the first time she heard the sofa farting.

Olive stands pencil-straight and crosses her heart. "Absolutely, 100%, I'll never tell. I will hold your truth in a vault. To prove it, we'll make a pact. I'll tell you a secret of mine. Then we'll each have something on the other, so we're guaranteed neither of us will squeal."

"It's a blood oath, but for secrets," I say, thinking this is a pretty clever idea.

"I'll go first," she says. "My brother got in colossal trouble last year when he took the car without permission and drove hundreds of miles to a concert. My parents couldn't find him for a couple of days and went out of their minds. It was pure chaos for a while, and he flunked his senior year."

"I bet they punished him big time."

She lowers her voice, "They sent Michael to a special school, but my parents told their friends he's away at college. That's our family secret."

That IS major.

"Your turn," Olive says, and resumes her place on the floor.

"Uh...my...uh...my Dad. Died. A while back." Each word still hurts as it leaves my mouth.

"Wow, sorry. So, you moved because he died?"

"There is a connection, but my mom refuses to tell me the true reason why we had to move."

"How did your father die?"

"Um," I hesitate.

"Oh my." Olive's eyes grow huge in alarm. "Was he murdered?"

Even in my wild speculations, my mind didn't go there. My first thought had been that maybe Dad's heart stopped because he caught a rare disease on his recent business trip. Mom might've been protecting me in case he exposed us to the same incurable sickness. For a while, I felt I was on borrowed time until weeks passed and neither Mom or I got sick.

"No. Of course not," I say, "Um...I don't think so. His heart—"

She finishes my sentence. "Oh, he had a heart attack."

"Not exactly. My mom says his heart stopped."

"That's called a heart attack."

"No attack, just stopped," I explain.

"You mean he was minding his own business, and his heart stopped? How can that happen?"

"Makes no sense. No one will tell me what really happened."

"Sounds as if there's a lot you don't know. And you're okay with that?"

"No, I'm not."

"So, do something about it."

"Like what?"

"A lot, Rocket Man. You should learn your family's truth. I can be your sous sleuth and help you solve this mystery."

"What's a sous sleuth?"

"Like a sous chef, an assistant. I'll be the assistant detective."

I'm not sure what she has in mind, but I check my phone and see that I have to get going.

"This will have to wait," I say. "I've got to change for soccer practice. Can you walk me to my grandfather's house? Otherwise, I'll be wandering around Milton for hours trying to find it."

"No prob, New Boy."

On the way, I say, "Hey, that trading secrets idea of yours is semi-brilliant. Have you done that before?"

"Can you believe it? I made it up on the spot. It isn't semi-brilliant; it's totally genius. I'll have to patent it." She stretches her arm way around her shoulder to pat herself on the back.

"I agree."

While we walk, Olive shares her funny teacher nicknames with me. There's Mother Malone and Handsome Handler. I keep up my end of the banter discussing my geography challenges and plans to embed a GPS chip in my arm so I can communicate with the satellites without interference and bypass the cell phone.

We part at the corner. Once I'm inside the house, Dad's voice pipes up. OLIVE'S NICE.

Was he with me at Olive's? That's wrong on so many levels.

Dad continues, BUDDY, IT'S GREAT OLIVE'S GOING TO HELP YOU.

"Can you please stay out of my business? Stop spying on me, especially when I'm with Olive." My voice comes out way harsher than I mean it. What kind of a kid uses that tone to his dead father?

CHAPTER 1

I change into shorts, soccer socks and cleats and debate whether to wear my Whitman Storm team shirt to practice, but decide a plain black one would be the smarter choice. I stuff the Whitman uniform into a corner of my soccer bag, along with my fabulous neon yellow goalie gloves, which cost a fortune. Mom had a fit about another extravagance, but Dad made her let me keep them. It'll be more bad luck if my new team already has their goalies lined up.

I expect the car ride with Grandpa will be super quiet until Grandpa actually speaks. "Did I tell you Skyline Park's soccer fields were built on the town's old landfill?"

"Are you kidding?" I say. "I'm playing soccer on top of heaps of garbage." I should've brought nose plugs instead of gloves.

Grandpa continues, elaborating on this strange piece of news.

"They capped and treated the landfill to prevent toxins from leaching out and topped it off with the best sod. I'd never let my grandson play on a field that wasn't absolutely safe. Wait until you see the place. The fields are beautiful."

That's an unusual amount of talking from Grandpa which is a sure sign he's super excited about this old dump. He parks, and we walk together toward a group on the far left. A powerful grassy smell fills my nose. I suck it in. Grandpa's right; these fields are perfect.

Grandpa introduces himself to the coach and then heads for the bleachers. I hope he brought a blanket to sit on or his butt will be frozen numb from those metal seats. It may be close to spring, but this winter in Massachusetts is still a frost-zone.

The coach says, "Ronald or Ron?"

"Rocky," I answer. "I mean, call me Rocky."

"Rocky it is. Your grandfather said you played goalie on your old team. We already have two kids sharing that position. Would you be willing to try offense?"

"Okay." Not arguing with the coach is a rule wherever you play, but I'm sure offense will be a fiasco. Goalie's my sweet spot. It defines me. Playing offense takes stamina. I hope my heart is in better shape than my dad's was.

Coach directs me to a group dribbling the ball side-to-side and up and down the field around a line of orange cones. My stomach aches as if I swallowed the soccer ball instead of having it between my feet. I'm desperate to make a good impression when my turn comes.

Corralling the ball and shifting it from one foot to the other, I jog downfield. Within a few seconds, my feet tangle, and I wind up face down in the dirt. A kid snickers, but nobody laughs out loud. Storm also didn't allow teammates to rag on each other. Still, I'm embarrassed. I stand up, find the ball that escaped and restart the drill.

Next up, we have to practice shooting, and a kid says, "Follow me," extending his hand for a fist bump.

"Hi, I'm Rocky," I say, completing the bump.

"Marco."

This drill might go better because goalies are strong kickers, but not always so good with our aim. My first shot sends the ball far over the net. On my second attempt, it veers wide left. Marco tells me to kick with the side of my cleat. Next time, the ball bounces on the ground in front of the goal, a modest improvement.

After practice, Coach says he's putting me on offense for now. Crappity, crapola. He hands Grandpa papers with information how to order a uniform and a copy of the team's schedule. It's official. I'm no longer the goalie for Whitman Storm. I'm a lousy, clumsy offensive player for the Milton Tigers.

We stop for takeout on the way home. When we pull up to the house, Mom's waiting for us.

"How's the new team?" she asks as soon as we're halfway inside. She's eager for good news. I bet she's dying for me to say it was great, or I'm thrilled not to have to play goalie anymore, or my new teammates are already my best friends so she can lose her guilt for dragging me away from Storm.

"Coach put me on offense," I answer, removing my shin guards and socks.

"That could be fun," she says, hoping I'll say sure, and she can pretend I'm okay with the move and everything, but she doesn't deserve to be let off after what she's done.

"The pressure on strikers to score is intense, and I'm never gonna get to wear my gloves again."

She exhales in a long sigh. I succeed in dashing any hopes she had that I'm happy with my new position. Now that she's down for the count, it might be a good time to ask her again to sign me up for the summer soccer clinic.

"I could amp up my game if you let me go to Whitman this summer for soccer."

"No. Not this summer," she says.

I have, once again, brought her to the verge of tears. I'm not a monster, but she's ruining my life. I lay it on thicker. "You are so unfair."

Anger leaks out from between my clenched teeth. I'm on a roll, and I don't let up on her. "Maybe you're worried that an intense week of soccer is too much for my heart."

"Where did that ridiculous idea come from?"

"Well, Dad was healthy, and his heart stopped, so maybe mine will too."

"It will NOT. Your heart works fine. You are totally healthy." She reaches for my hand, but I pull it away.

"Why should I trust you?" I say, taking off upstairs without waiting for her answer. I said that to annoy her. I wasn't seriously worried that my heart is bad. I always get checked around my birthday, and the doctor tells me I'm perfect.

While I'm in the shower, the not-a-ghost dad says emphatically, APOLOGIZE TO YOUR MOM.

Can he order me around? Are there any rules in this kind of situation?

I wrap myself in a towel.

Dad doesn't let up. MOM'S DOING HER BEST. YOU SHOULD KNOW THAT.

Okay, now I feel like a skunk.

I put on my jeans as a text comes in from Olive: Meet me by the green monster doors tomorrow before homeroom. I've planned a plan.

CHAPTER 8

I leave for school earlier than usual and catch sight of Olive hanging out with some girls. When she spots me, she moves to the side so we can talk in private.

"Do you know Ms. Malone?" she asks.

"Yeah, I talked to her once."

"Wow. Already. They're not taking any chances with you. Last year, when my family went a little manic, they made me go see her a few times. She always has the kid's folder on her desk when she meets with you. Maybe the answers are in there."

"Those files are top secret. She won't let me look inside my folder."

"Who said anything about asking for permission? She would

probably throw a bazillion questions at you to find out why you want to see your file. We have to get you alone with your folder."

"That's impossible."

"Think outside-the-box, Rocket Man. Here's the plan. Make an appointment with her, and after a little while, I'll barge in with a made-up emergency. Malone will come with me. While she's out, you read as much as you can. You may not have long."

"We could get into trouble."

"We won't."

How can she be positive?

Dad whispers not to be afraid. He was always devising ways to cure me of my fears. Once, he made me ride a roller coaster all day long until I was dizzy and nauseous. I went to bed without dinner. Mom told me after that I should use my head too when Dad wants to do something that seems too over-the-top.

Olive says, "Make an appointment soon, and tell me when it is."

With Dad on Olive's side, it's two against one. I say, "Okay. I'm in."

The plan is on.

I HEAD STRAIGHT for Ms. Malone's office before homeroom. Her door is open; I walk in.

She's surprised to see me. "Is everything okay, Rocky?"

"Er...," I stutter and picture myself with tiny beady eyes, sharp fang-teeth and a long rat-tail for fooling nice Ms. Malone. "Uh...I want to change my Social Studies class," I explain. "Mr. Handler insists I have to learn where all these crazy places are, something like Moronoco. He's on my case."

"Let's talk about it." She opens her calendar. "I'm busy this morning. Can you come right after lunch?"

"Today?" I didn't expect the appointment so soon. I swallow a big bite of air. Olive won't have much time to prepare, but I have no excuse for postponing it. This could be a recipe for failure cake. I forgot the cardinal rule: school counselors are deliriously happy when kids want to come voluntarily. Ms. Malone's no exception. I probably made her day, and she seized onto this fantastic opportunity in case it never happens again.

"Yes," she says, "we'll take care of this and make sure you're in the right class."

"Okay." What if Olive isn't ready today?

SHE WILL BE, Dad says, OLIVE CAN HANDLE THIS. I resent his confidence while I'm steeling myself against a potential disaster.

YOU WORRY TOO MUCH, the not-a-ghost dad says.

"I do not." My voice fills the empty hallway.

"Who are you talking to?" That's not Dad's voice, and it's coming from behind me. A second ago, I was totally alone. I turn. It's Max; he snuck up on me.

This is bad. "Clean out your earwax, Shrek," I say. "I'm practicing my lines for a piece I had to memorize for Language Arts."

"I don't believe that. You were talking to some imaginary person. Maybe I should tell Ms. Malone you have little pretend friends. She sends kids like you to a special school," he snorts.

"Leave me alone."

Max does the two fingers to his eyes in the classic I'm-watching-you motion, and then leaves.

It will be a catastrophe if he tells anyone he caught me talking to no one.

CHAPTER 9

I'm panicked that I won't see Olive until lunch, and she'll have zero time to get ready. When I spy her in the food line, she motions to me to cut in front of her.

"After lunch," I whisper.

"Huh?" she grunts, as she puts milk and chips on her tray.

OMG, did she forget the plan already?

"Ms. Malone." I say, trying to kickstart her memory.

Her eyes jump in delight like two hi-bounce balls. "Fantastic. We're on!" She's says, rubbing her hands together with a mischievous smile. She's a professional at this stuff. Me, I'm dreading this more than a dozen flu shots in one day.

We find our usual table, and Olive says, "Obvs, you must work fast once I get her out."

"I plan to photo each page and read them when there's more time."

"Excellent idea." She points a finger at my head. "You've got some brains, Rocket Man."

The bell ending the lunch period rings, and I make my way to Ms. Malone's office-closet. Columns of invisible ants march up and down my skin, making the nerves in my arms tingle. My stomach informs me having the supposed "chicken cacciatore" today might have been a mistake. I could leave my own personal contribution for the custodian on Tucker's floor.

REMEMBER WHAT I TOLD YOU, Dad says, "IF YOU TAKE A RISK, YOU MIGHT... He always paused there, waiting for me to end his sentence with a loud, joyful "Succeed!" It was so barf-worthy.

I raise my fist to knock on Ms. Malone's door, and at that exact moment she pulls it open. I come within inches of landing a punch. She ignores that I almost bopped her and invites me to sit down with her warm, smooth honey voice.

She opens my folder and takes out a copy of my schedule. "Rocky, whatever the problem is with Social Studies, I'm sure we can fix it."

She's way too nice. I'm a turd for doing this to her. The only thing I've got going for me is the glimmer of truth in what I'm about to say which means I can avoid telling a total lie. Still, I don't meet her eyes.

"It's geography. I've never had it before. I'm no good at it." I drag out each word to give Olive more time.

"Maybe you'll surprise yourself," Ms. Malone suggests.

"And not only is it difficult, it's pretty useless too." I glance up at her for a minute, as she removes her glasses and lets them dangle around her neck. She flashes an eye twinkle in my direction.

"Why is it useless?" she asks.

"Well, nowadays, there are free GPS apps for your phone. Do you know what that is, Ms. Malone?" This isn't me being a wise guy. Sometimes old people don't have a clue what global positioning is, and if you mention Instagram or Snapchat, most adults sink into confusion. I continue, "Mr. Handler is so gung-ho about maps like they are the only way to learn —"

The door flings open. Olive bursts in completely out of breath. She must have raced up and down the stairs a few times to make it realistic.

"Ms. Malone," she huffs, "sorry to bother you, but two boys are fighting near the auditorium. Come quick, before the little guy gets killed!"

I'm on the verge of cracking up at her performance. I bend down and pretend to retie my sneaker so Ms. Malone can't see my face. I peek up as Ms. Malone is grabbing her two-way radio. She flies out after Olive. As soon as they're gone, I whip out my phone and pull out the papers in the folder. I finish photographing them fast and shove my phone in my jeans' pocket.

Adrenaline is pumping in me, and my heart flings itself against my chest so hard it hurts. I'm drenched and grab a tissue off Ms. Malone's desk to sop up my wet forehead. It must be a counselor-rule to always have tissues at the ready for crying kids like I was when I first went after Dad died. If the counselor mentioned "your dad," I lost it. It took me a while to get that under control. Now, when tears search for an exit, I tighten my eyes to prevent their escape. That method works if you're fast enough to catch the liquid before it spills out.

I throw my used tissue in the wastebasket and notice a sheet of paper on the floor. I must've dropped it in my rush. Now there's a dirty imprint of my sneaker on the copy of my sixth-grade report card. I stick it into the way back of the folder and pray Ms. Malone never looks for it.

This is taking too long. Ms. Malone should've returned already. Olive could be sitting in the principal's office this minute, and if she's caught, so am I.

Finally, Ms. Malone walks in. I try to hold my expression in neutral and not give myself away. She appears flustered and stares at the folder for a minute. Yikes, I didn't pay attention to its exact position on the table when she left. Is it facing in the same direction? I'd make a lousy criminal. Panic rises in me like vomit. I attempt to swallow it down.

Ms. Malone says, "Sorry for the interruption, Rocky. When I got to the auditorium, the kids had gone. Olive has no idea who they are. Nothing can be done unless one of the boys reports to the office or to the nurse. I'm glad she came to find the nearest adult. Fights in school are never tolerated. Now, let's see what we can do about your Social Studies class."

She pulls the folder closer to her.

CHAPTER 10

Before Ms. Malone opens my folder, a torrent of words pours from my mouth. "I reconsidered the whole thing while you were gone. I should give it more time with Mr. Handler because he's helping me to catch up which is nice of him."

Ms. Malone beams. I stand and sling my backpack onto my shoulder, preparing to scram.

"That's a mature attitude, Rocky. Mr. Handler is dedicated. You'll like him, even if geography isn't one of your favorites. There's a lot of adjustment with new teachers and new kids. Have you made some friends yet?"

"Not really," I answer. Even a five-year-old would have the smarts not to mention Olive at this particular moment.

"You will. Keep a positive outlook, and everything will fall into place. Come here anytime you want to talk."

"Okay." And I'm out the door, repeating a silent prayer she never opens that folder.

Ms. Malone will never notice one paper out of place. You worry too much, Dad says.

The not-a-ghost dad cannot know that any more than I do, and I do NOT.

Naturally, I can't be sure, Dad responds to my unspoken comment. There could be a problem. And don't mention that paper to Olive. No reason for that.

He's invaded my mind on a permanent basis, but I agree with him. I hate not to tell Olive the truth, but I don't want her to think I'm a total screw-up.

I slip into a corner between two rows of lockers to hide while I text Olive a thumbs up emoji. She won't check her phone until last bell. Getting caught with your phone out during class breaks the "no phones" rule. You can lose it for three days. No kid will risk that.

My phone pings at 3:00. Olive could win an Olympic gold for speedy texters. She sends a big old smiley face emoji.

I reply with the same.

She texts: did you read?

Me: not yet

Olive: come over. don't read alone - in case??????

Me: will ask

I'm pretty confident Mom will agree since it's like in the parents' handbook not to refuse a request to go to a friend's if it's to do schoolwork. I text Mom, and within a minute, she gives me the okay.

I head for the meeting corner a couple of blocks from school. I arranged this spot with Olive because I don't want us to wind up on the Tucker rumor track. Olive thought it was kind of ridiculous, but I insisted.

On the walk to her house, Olive gives me the deets on how it went on her end when Ms. Malone followed her to find the pretend kids.

Looking pleased with herself, she says, "It worked perfectly. I knew it would."

Then she adds, "Hope Ms. Malone doesn't lie awake nights guessing who the two boys are."

I detect a hint of guilt in her too about Ms. Malone. I follow Olive inside as she calls to her mom to alert her that she brought me with her again.

Even without advance notice, Olive's mom is able to whip up a bunch of goodies for us in no time. She's a snack-master professional.

In the family room, I notice a photo on the small table near the sofa. It's of Olive and a boy, who is even taller than she is. She's smiley, and he looks as if his dog just ran away.

"Is that your brother?" I ask and join her on the floor instead of risking the crackling sounds of the sofa.

"Yeah, that's Michael. He's awesome. I haven't seen him in forever. They don't allow phones at his school. Once a week, he calls my parents from the office, but it's always when I'm not home. I miss him." Her eyes drop, and she gets quiet.

It might be better if I avoid the subject of her brother. Too sensitive.

A minute later she raises her face and says, "So, Rocket Man, it's time."

CHAPTER 11

T he words "it's time" stick in my throat. I gulp and reach for my phone and place my finger on the camera icon.

The first photo is a registration form with the usual name, address and emergency contact information. Under Father's name, the word "deceased," and the date he died glare up at me. The next one is a letter from the guidance counselor at my old school. I read her note:

> Until his father's death, Ronald's (we call him Rocky) work was quite good. He participated in classes and was conscientious about his homework. He has lots of friends, especially the boys on his soccer team.
>
> His transcript demonstrates that he is capable of maintaining a high average. However, the last quarter he had trouble focusing, and

there was a downturn in his grades. The sudden loss of his father was extremely difficult for Rocky, as it would be for any child.

Right after the death, his attendance was erratic for a while, and his grades started to slip. His mother decided they needed to change their surroundings as quickly as possible, and she didn't want to wait until the end of the school year. I hope the transition to Tucker isn't too disruptive for Rocky, as he copes with his grief.

Please call me if you have any questions or concerns.
Sincerely,
Belle Clark, MEd, School Counselor

The rest of the photos are copies of my grades, which weren't too bad until they went into the toilet after Dad died.

I put my phone down. "Nothing new. Nada. Zippo. A bunch of useless forms, report cards and a letter from my old guidance counselor who also thought we left Whitman in a big hurry."

"That's important, isn't it?" Olive asks, grasping at that shred of information in the hope our stunt won't have been a complete bust.

"Not so much."

"We'll need to get more creative," Olive says, "this mystery won't solve itself."

She rebounds fast, but then again, this isn't about *her* father.

Go to Whitman, Dad says with his one-track mind.

"But how?" I ask Dad, again forgetting to speak only inside my head. If I don't get that under control, I'm gonna get caught in a heap of trouble. But it's more natural to respond out loud.

Olive answers, "I don't know yet."

Saved again because my question could work for both Olive and Dad.

Dad repeats Olive's line, I don't know how yet.

Dealing with the two of them at once is like being double-teamed.

"Do you want to walk me home?" I ask Olive, "You don't have to."

She winks at me, and says, "So, you've learned the geography of our neighborhood. There's hope for you. But I'll keep you company. We can plot on the way."

Olive, ever the optimist.

By the time I get to Grandpa's, my disappointment is growing faster than a wayward beanstalk on steroids. I had hoped that, by now, I'd have found the truth.

I'm already upset at dinner, and then Mom lobs a thunderbolt in my direction. "Invite Olive for dinner next week. I'd love to meet her."

The scene of Mom, Grandpa, Olive and me around the table is an appetite killer. Mom better not be imagining Olive's my girlfriend, which she is NOT. Mom always wants to meet my friends, but Olive IS different.

I'm not saying yes until Mom agrees to something I want. I ask, "Shawn's birthday is in a couple of weeks. Can I go?" His parties are always cooler than cool.

"It's a long drive, and I have extra work on the weekends."

Grandpa says, "I can drive him. I don't mind."

I almost leap to my feet to hug him for coming to my rescue, until Mom says with a slight scold, "Pop, he's not going. You aren't helping."

"Dad would let me," I say, and immediately composition-paper lines mark Mom's forehead and her eyes droop as if little weights are dragging the lids down. Okay, that wasn't nice of me, but I don't owe her nice now.

Mom sounds weary like she finished a ten-mile hike. She speaks slowly. "If Dad was here, a lot would be different, but he isn't. Enough. I can't do this with you."

"You're not gonna let me see my Whitman friends ever again, are you?" Scorching fire shoots from my nostrils aimed directly at her.

"They'll be at the playoff game this Sunday."

If she thinks seeing Shawn and the guys for a few minutes at the game is the same as going to his party, she has lost her mind.

"That doesn't count," I say. "I'm not on their team and can't even talk to them on the bench."

"End of discussion."

I leave the table and clang my plate against the side of the sink, breaking off a small chunk of the rim. Mom can add another transgression to her growing list of my sins.

In my room, I retrieve the soccer clinic application from my desk and begin to fill it out even though I'm sure she'll never let me go to dreaded Whitman. I pause when I get to the line where a parent or guardian has to sign.

Dad says, WHOA, ROCKY, FORGING A SIGNATURE IS A BIG DEAL. THERE WOULD BE SEVERE CONSEQUENCES IF YOU'RE CAUGHT.

"But I'm desperate to go. You said if I went and trained hard, I'd make varsity in high school and maybe score a scholarship to college. Mom would like that, wouldn't she?

THINGS CHANGE, he says.

They sure do. I put the form back into its envelope without committing any crimes. After stuffing it in my desk drawer, I text Shawn.

Me: playoffs Milton versus Whitman

Shawn: Weird. Right?

Me: you know it. things change

I use the exact same words Dad said to me a second ago.

Me: I play offense

Shawn: No way

Me: way

I get another incoming text, so I sign off with Shawn.

Olive: New plan?

Me: Not yet

She sends a sad emoji face

Me: mom wants you to come for dinner

Olive: Great.

She adds a thumbs up emoji.

This is no problem for her. For me, it's like I drank Ipe-something, the stuff that makes you have to throw up.

BECAUSE YOU LIKE HER, Dad says.

Double, triple Ugh.

CHAPTER 12

Playoff Sunday rolls in with perfect soccer weather, just enough chill so you don't overheat. Normally, I'd be pumped for such a big game, but having to play against old teammates is kinda messed up. I should be wearing a Storm Red shirt today and not this bluish-green color Mom refers to as "cute." Soccer shirts are not cute.

We all are silent in the car driving to the field. Neither Mom or I have seen Whitman people since we moved. It will be weird for sure. Mom parks, and I dash to the side of the field where Storm players are warming up. This might be a mistake because today Storm's my enemy. I slap Shawny on the back, not too hard, just hard enough. He punches me on the arm.

"I'll go easy on you, Roc," Shawn jokes.

Another guy joins in. "Hey, Rocky, are you spying on us? This is a private team area. Out!"

"But I wanted to—" I start to explain. Before I finish my sentence, the guys burst out laughing. I can't believe I'm so out of the loop I don't pick up on their teasing. I'm an outsider with my old buddies.

Then Jacoby says, "Let's kidnap him," grabbing my arm.

I pull away. "Gotta go. Good luck," I call out as I jog to the Tigers' side of the field, hoping my new team doesn't take me for a traitor.

I don't want Storm to win without me as their goalie, but rooting against my friends is low. Once again, leaving Whitman bites me, creating problems I never had when Shawn and I were on the same team.

The first half of the game is gruesome. After twenty minutes of running up and down the field, Coach pulls me out to catch my breath and drink. Goalies never get winded, and I was only taken out of a game once when I dove for a block and landed hard. That day, Dad ran onto the field even though parents are forbidden to do that. He made a big scene complaining about the lack of defense, and Coach sent me home, even though I was fine.

Dad could create a commotion at my games, shouting from the stands and embarrassing me in front of the coach and my teammates. But I wish he was here today cheering me on even if he goes overboard.

Coach hustles us onto the field for the second half. I try to push Dad out of my mind and get my head back in the game. I run out alongside Tan, who plays goalie second half, until Coach pulls me to the side and says, "You're holding back, Rocky. When you have an opportunity, shoot. Don't pass it."

"Okay," I say. He could tell I've been dodging shots all game. I'm afraid of looking klutzy.

As I move into position on the field, Dad's voice calls after me, KNOW WHERE THE BALL IS. FEEL IT BETWEEN YOUR FEET. KEEP YOUR EYE ON THE NET AND KICK IT LOW INTO THE CORNER. Then he adds, Can't wait to get a load of Shawn's face when you make a goal.

"Fat chance of me scoring," I mutter under my breath and glance into the stands, expecting to see Dad there, giving me the double thumbs-up. When Dad missed a couple of really important games because of his stupid business trips, I was pretty bratty and didn't talk to him for a whole week.

Most of the second half of the game, I luck out and am nowhere near taking a shot. We're tied with Storm, and the clock shows ten minutes left. Marco passes to me, and Shawn moves in to steal the ball, taunting me with trash talk.

I do a few quick dribbles and race down the field. No Stormers get even close. When I'm inside the goal box, I kick. Once the ball's in the air, my right foot swings out from under me as I go butt first onto the turf. I pop up in Dash-like speed, praying no one noticed my clumsiness. I turn toward the net in time to catch sight of the ball sailing in. Goal!

There's loud cheering from the stands as I run up the field. I high-five Marco on the way and pat the curls on the top of his head. Tan is clapping. The Storm guys look stunned. They've only seen me play goalie. Even Shawn hasn't put a point on the board today.

I taste victory if we can hold on. We do. It's sweet until I have to line up and slap hands on the opposite side from my old friends. From the first whistle, this game has been as overwhelming as my life since the moment Dad died. I'm glad it's in the history books.

I pack up my gear and head for the bleachers, spotting Mom huddled with Shawn's mother at the far end of an empty row. Mom's wiping her eyes. Like a sneaky cat, I detour and go under the bleachers, close enough to eavesdrop.

Mom says, "He's hoping we might move back. We can't. Not yet."

"Too risky. Too soon," Ms. R. says.

Risky how? Is Mom involved in something in Whitman? She couldn't be. We were away when Dad died, and she was genuinely in shock when she found out. It doesn't make sense.

"I guess you're right, Rochelle. But part of me wishes I could tell him the truth now."

"You will know when you want to tell him," Ms. R. says and hugs Mom. They stay wrapped together for a while. I leave my spot and circle around so Mom won't suspect I was listening.

Ms. R. spots me and says hello in a way-too-loud voice to alert Mom to my presence as any good co-conspirator would do.

Mom turns around and comes face-to-face with me. The whites of her eyes glow at me.

Dad says, ROCKY, CHECK YOUR OVERACTIVE IMAGINATION. THERE IS NO WEIRD STUFF HAPPENING IN WHITMAN. DRY ERASE YOUR BRAIN.

Dad, maybe you're wrong. In any case, you have no answers so how would you know?

Ms. R. says, "Great game, Rocky. You're as good on offense as you were as goalie."

Mom gives me a quick hug and whispers, "Dad would be so proud of you. You did great."

"Right, I did." I don't mention Dad was giving me pointers today. Mom has her secrets, so I'm keeping mine.

"Like I always say, remember the wonderful things," Mom says.

Parents can drive you bonkers. Mom makes us leave Whitman where I have lots of memories of Dad, and then every chance she gets, she tells me to remember him.

As we walk to the car, I decide to probe Mom if she ever did anything she shouldn't have. I ask her, "Did you ever break a law?"

"What a strange question. Years ago, I got a ticket for speeding. When the policeman pulled me over, my knees were clanging against each other in warp speed. I couldn't breathe. It took me days to recover."

"Did you have to get a lawyer and go to court?"

"No, I paid the ticket and was careful never to go more than five miles over the speed limit. They give you a tiny bit of leeway."

My theory of her doing something wrong is turning out to be a dud. Mom's no criminal.

"How was it seeing Whitman people?" I ask her.

"Nice, actually. Rochelle won a major Own Voices Award for her book. I'm glad I got to congratulate her in person."

"Can we visit sometime?" I'm curious if today changes anything.

"Not now."

If I could find out what she's scared of, maybe I can help fix it and prove to Mom it's safe for us in Whitman. I've got to keep trying.

If Shawn's mom told him the secret, he'd tell me, wouldn't he?

At Grandpa's, I call Shawn.

Shawn bellows, "Hey, what's up, man? You never call."

"Something important."

"I didn't mean what I said today. You've done your share of trash talk too."

"Calm down, Shawn. This has nothing to do with the game."

"So, what gives?"

"Did your mom ever say anything to you about how my dad died?"

"Huh?"

"Your mom knows some secret about my dad."

"All she says is she misses your mom."

"Swear."

"I swear," Shawn says.

"Can you sort of casual-like ask her how my dad died? You've got to be subtle. Say you were sad we had to move and ask if we left because of how my father died. Try to get some info. Do not tell your mom I asked you to do that."

"Promise." With Shawn, I don't need a secret pact. We're tight since kindergarten.

I press end.

Mom's secret has the jaws of a giant python, clamping down ready to swallow me whole.

CHAPTER 13

M onday mornings wouldn't be such a drag if school started on Tuesdays.

THAT MAKES NO SENSE, the not-a-ghost dad says, sounding as grumpy as I feel.

I shed my sweatpants for jeans and smell my t-shirt to decide if it is wearable today, but it's offensive. As I swap it out for a clean one, I explain to Dad, "It's a joke. It wouldn't work. If we start school on Tuesdays, we'd have to go on Saturdays, and no one wants to go to school on the weekend. And why do you sound upset today?"

SAME REASON AS YOU.

"That's ridiculous. I'm the person who's living in a lie, not you. Why do you insist on keeping this a secret too? You're as bad as Mom."

I UNDERSTAND THIS IS CONFUSING TO YOU. I WISH I COULD TELL YOU WHAT YOU WANT TO KNOW.

Same old, same old from him. Why do I even bother to ask? My breakfast stomach distracts me, shouting for food, and I go downstairs to heed its message.

"Good morning," Mom says. She's all cheery, unlike Dad and me. She and her secrets must be having a fabulous day together.

I say nothing and take down three boxes of cereal to mix a combo. At least now I can get stuff by myself and don't have to ask for everything.

"Mister, I said 'good morning.'"

I take a spoonful and chomp as loudly as I can to annoy her.

"What's with the attitude?" she asks. "You should be flying high this morning after that terrific score yesterday. You've only been playing offense for a short time."

I slide an envelope across the table toward her.

"What's this?"

"If my soccer is that important to you, then why don't you sign the application to the soccer clinic? It's here waiting for your signature." Because my luck has vanished on an around-the-world trip with no return ticket, forging her name was a leap I didn't dare make. I'd probably get caught and lose my phone, my bike and probably a ton of other stuff.

She doesn't even open the envelope and pushes it across the table toward me.

"Not this summer. Maybe the next one."

"Why should I believe you?" I sputter at her, causing cereal to spit out of my mouth as I grab the envelope.

She warns, "You'd better have a different tone tonight when Olive's here."

Yikes, I forgot she's coming for dinner. Could this day get any worse? And to top it off, I'm having my first test in Handsome Handler's class.

I wish it was Tuesday already.

I BREEZE through the first section of the social studies test, nailing all the questions, but my good fortune is short-lived when I face a tough fill-in.

The first explorer to reach the Pacific Ocean was _____ and he was from _____.

I studied this but can't remember the answer. I decide to ask a certain someone for help. I don't think this is actual cheating.

Hey, Dad, is the answer Magellan? I'm careful this time to keep my words inside my head.

GIVE ME A SEC TO THINK, he replies. I'm glad I'm the only who can hear him.

I move on to the next question.

Then Dad blurts out, BALBOA FROM SPAIN.

This is freaky amazing because the second he gives me the answer I remember it too. I write it in.

Thanks, Dad.

Then I block on a multiple-choice question, and ask him, *Who was the first non-native person to cross the Mississippi River? There are three choices—*

YOU DON'T HAVE TO READ THEM TO ME. I CAN SEE THEM.

How does he "see" the paper? He isn't a ghost with eyes, mouth and ears.

You knew the Balboa answer, I complain.

IT ISN'T SIR FRANCIS DRAKE FOR SURE. I'M STUCK BETWEEN HERNANDO DE SOTO OR PONCE DE LEON.

Phul-eeze.

NO CAN DO. TAKE A GUESS.

I circle De Soto, because I'm pretty sure that Ponce guy was in Florida trying to discover the fountain of youth. I'm the explorer who's seeking the fountain of truth. Ha. Ha. I think Olive would appreciate that joke.

After class, Olive asks how I did.

"Okay."

"Can't wait for tonight," she says, "I'm sure your mom will love me. You'll never guess what horrible thing I have to do this weekend."

"What?" I ask, having difficulty believing anything could be more awful than this dinner.

"Tell you on the way to your house."

Having dinner with Mom and Olive makes my brain spin in an out-of-control orbit. I wish Marco or another guy from soccer was coming tonight instead of Olive. If Mom had to insist I invite someone, I didn't want it to be her.

Dad explains, You DON'T WANT HER TO COME OVER BECAUSE SHE'S A GIRL.

Oh great, now you have the answer. Where were you when I needed help on the test?

CHAPTER 14

After school, I arrive first at Olive's and my arranged spot and sit on a nearby stone wall to wait for her.

Dad's voice says, HEY, DON'T WORRY SO MUCH ABOUT DINNER TONIGHT. BOY AND GIRL STUFF CAN BE COMPLICATED.

I do a quick check around me. I'm alone so I speak out loud.

"Mom's gonna embarrass me," I complain.

GIVE HER MORE CREDIT. AND REMEMBER TO USE THE 'ROCKY CHARM.'

Since I was five, Dad told me I had "Rocky charm", whatever that is. I always planned to ask him. I wonder if he could tell me now, or if it's too late.

Dad laughs. YOU'LL KNOW IT WHEN IT HAPPENS. MAYBE

GRANDPA WILL SAY MORE THAN A FEW GRUNTS AT DINNER TONIGHT.

This dinner might actually be even more of a disaster if Dad was there. He could be unpredictable at times and monopolize the conversation with fantastic stories. He claimed they were all true, but Mom said he had a robust imagination and some magical thinking.

WELL, I'M SORT OF GOING TO BE THERE, Dad says, BUT I GUESS I CAN'T EMBARRASS YOU ANYMORE.

He "heard" me. I didn't mean to make him sad. More than anything in the world I'd want the real him to be at dinner tonight even if he did tell an outrageous tale.

I'm about to apologize, but then the not-a-ghost dad says, YOU AND OLIVE ARE QUITE THE TEAM.

I can almost "see" him grinning which gives me a sickening feeling.

I shout, "Olive is off limits. No comments about her."

ARE YOU GOING TO KISS HER? he asks.

Whoa! Where did that come from? This is super embarrassing. I have zero privacy in my head. I wish I could boot him out of there, or at least make him knock before he entered.

Then he says, YOU SHOULD HOLD HANDS WITH HER WHEN YOU WALK HOME, BUT ASK HER FIRST IF IT'S OKAY.

I picture Dad smiling and pushing his big, black-framed glasses to the top of his head. This always revealed his roaming left eye veering off-center with a happy twinkle. That dancing eye would hypnotize me, but there were other times when his eyes could look hollow, almost disappearing into deep, dark caves.

"No, I'm not doing that!" I yell. "Gross."

A boisterous laugh breaks the air behind me. As I swing around to see who's there, I'm almost afraid that this time I'll come face-to-face with my dead father. It's Max, a professional stalker. He sports a big, fat clown grin that shows off a mouth full of blue and silver metal. My stinkin' luck is in full bloom.

"What the heck is wrong with you?" Max demands.

He's stealthy like a plane flying under the radar to avoid detection. The best move I can make now is to go on offense. I try to keep my voice from wavering and say, "What are you talking about?" I pretend I have no clue what he's referring to.

"Do you always argue with yourself or did one of those goblins that run around in your head mouth off? Want me to beat them up for you?"

Max moves in closer. I raise my fist and rest it so it practically touches his nose. I've never been in a fight in my whole life. The guys and I fool around, pretending to box, without hitting anyone for real. I only want to scare Max away. I'm like a slab of iron stuck in his magnetic grasp, and he won't release me.

"Well, Fartface, I think Ms. Malone should be informed about your little problem."

"Max, give me a break. Don't tell her anything."

"And what'll you do to shut me up?"

"What do you want?"

"I'll come up with something big, Fartmeister."

He takes off, as Olive jogs up. "Sorry I'm late," she says. "Was that Max? What's the matter? Your face looks sunburnt, which is pretty much impossible in March in New England."

"Maybe I'm coming down with a cold," I suggest and suck in deep breaths of cold air to lower my body temperature, hoping my normal color returns.

"Are you sick?" she asks.

"It's nothing."

"Doesn't seem like nothing."

"It's Max," I say.

"What about him?"

"He's giving me a hard time."

"Does Max know your dad died?" Olive asks.

"No."

"Because I swear I didn't tell anyone."

"I trust you. Max heard something he shouldn't."

"What?"

"I'll explain later," I say, but maybe I won't. Telling someone you talk to your dead father could make them run far, far away.

"So, did you win your game yesterday?" Olive changes the subject.

"Since when are you a soccer fan?"

"I'm not. Not really. So, did you?"

"I scored once." I wish I had that gorgeous kick on video.

"Well, la-de-da for you, but you should totally play hockey instead. It'd be perfect. I'd call you Rocky Hockey."

Olive could launch a company selling nicknames. She'd make a fortune.

"Ha. Ha. Very funny."

Olive says, "I'm bummed. My dad insists on taking me camping this weekend so I can collect real specimens for my science report. He wants me to get an A, but really he needs to keep busy because he misses my brother."

"What's wrong with camping? It's super fun."

"Boys. So typical. For me, sleeping in a cramped tent, surrounded by bugs and other creepy-crawly things with my snoring old father is worse than the dentist filling a mouthful of cavities without Novocain. If you love camping so much, he should take you instead."

"That wouldn't work."

"Joking, Rocket Man. Chill."

"Camping is wonderful. I went all the time with my dad and uncle."

"I will not like it!" Olive makes my eardrums almost burst.

"Poor you," I say with a dose of sarcasm.

"An uncle?" she asks, "Does he know the truth about your dad?"

"He was with my dad the day it happened. They were close brothers."

"Why don't you ask him for answers?"

"Mom would get suspicious if I wanted to see him alone, plus he travels a lot."

"Rocky, sometimes you give up too easily. Nothing is impossible. We'll figure out something."

When we get to the front door, I take out the key Grandpa gave me a couple of days ago and bring Olive into the den to meet him. He picks his head up from the book and says hello, but nothing more. Obviously, he doesn't want to exhaust his word supply before dinner.

Olive and I microwave some popcorn, fill two glasses with lemonade and head upstairs, because no one told me Olive couldn't be in my room. But then again, I never asked.

Olive takes a spot on the floor, as usual. She could live in a world without chairs. She crosses her legs, and her knees poke out of the holes in her jeans. With lightning speed, she removes her ponytail holder, grabs her hair and redoes it. No mirror. Amazing. I sit on my bed.

Olive says, "I've got it! I astonish myself sometimes with my brilliance. You're lucky to have such a loyal, smart, awesome friend like me. Here's the deal: Tell your mom you have a science project too and need to collect specimens. She'll let you go camping if she's convinced you'll get a better grade. Parents always agree to that type of stuff."

"Are you kidding? I'm not camping with you."

She roars, "Not with me. That's too funny. With your uncle, obvs. Camping would give you two time alone, away from your mom. You could give him the third degree."

"But I don't have that assignment."

"Duh. So what? You've never lied before?"

"Sure, I have," I answer with bravado, but I don't lie, at least not to Mom. Not yet.

Dad butts in. It might work, and it's only a little lie. My own father is encouraging me to fib to Mom. This moment should be enshrined as history-making.

I repeat the not-a-ghost dad's words, "Might work."

"We're on. We'll set it up during dinner tonight. Follow my lead."

"Uh," I stammer.

"Now what?"

"Uh, I've got another problem." I feel an invisible hand drawing a big letter "L" on my forehead.

"Spit it out already. You are trouble central," she says.

"It's Max."

"What about him?"

"He's blackmailing me."

CHAPTER 15

Olive tilts her head and gazes at me with the same confused expression I get when I have to face a ridiculously hard math problem. No one cares what time trains arrive at the station with different speeds from different directions. It's not as if I'm in training to be a conductor.

She asks, "What are you doing that Max can blackmail you? You do NOT want to owe him anything."

Now I'll have to unload my hugest, most heavy-duty secret. This could be a ginormous mistake I'll regret for the rest of my life. But if I want her help, I have no choice.

I say, "Swear not to tell a word of this to anyone."

Her lips press together, and her eyes narrow to half slits. She looks annoyed. "Why would you even say that? Our secret oath is still operating."

Dad whispers to me he has confidence in Olive, but he doesn't know her any better than I do, so his opinion on that score is pretty much worthless.

My armpits are soggy wet, as I plunge in and say, "My dad talks to me."

Olive's eyes morph from bewildered to surprised. "What did you say?" she asks as if I'm speaking Martian.

"You heard me," I say. "Don't jump to conclusions. I'm not having visions. He talks to me, gives me advice and makes comments. That's it."

"Can you see him?" She scans the room, probably imagining he's hanging around here. I still do that too sometimes.

"No. He's a voice, but not a ghost. He doesn't jump out of the closet in the middle of the night and shout 'Boo.'"

I study her to see if she plans to bolt for the door after this revelation. Our friendship could be skating on cracked ice, ready to dump us into the freezing water. I suck in my chest wall as much as I can and hold my breath waiting to find out how she'll react.

A long time passes before she says, "So, since he died, he's been talking to you?"

"No, only after we moved here."

"Why?" she asks.

"Because I'm upset we had to leave Whitman, and I'm desperate for the truth. He says he wants to help me."

"That makes sense, I guess. Do you hate it when he talks to you?"

"At first, hearing his voice inside my head terrified me, but I got used to it. Mostly, I like him hanging around, except when he's butting into my personal stuff."

"Ha, he's the same as all parents! Tell him hi for me the next time you speak to him."

And with that, I re-expand my chest. She has no judgment on me.

"I will." I can't help but smile. Only someone like Olive would understand that smiling while I'm thinking about my dead father at the same time doesn't make me a bad person.

"Did you tell your mom?" she asks.

"No way. She'd freak."

"Yeah, she would. Parents are quick to ring the alarm, imagining every little thing their kid does can affect their whole life and ought to be put under the microscope. To me, you seem like a regular kid, or am I wrong?" A sly grin flashes from her mouth.

"Definitely regular," I agree.

"So, what does this have to do with Max?"

"He caught me talking to my dad once or twice when I thought I was alone and spoke out loud by mistake. My bad. Now he's threatening to tell Ms. Malone and get me sent to some special school. Ms. Malone will tell my mom for sure, and then I'll be in the counselor's office forever explaining why this isn't a problem."

"Could Max hear your dad too?"

"Only me."

At that moment, Olive sits up straight and stares past me. I turn around and see Mom walking in. She doesn't have to knock today, because I left the door open. She says hi to Olive and glances to the corner where I stack my dirty clothes. They're out-of-sight. I'd never leave used boxers on display in front of Olive. After a bit of chatter, Mom excuses herself to finish cooking.

Once Mom's gone, Olive says, "As Handsome Handler, master of globes, says 'back to topic.' I'll negotiate with Max for you and find out what he wants for his silence."

"Really?" I'm beyond grateful. Olive is more than a geography partner.

"You'll owe me for this."

Yikes, I hope I didn't escape one problem for another. Olive's mind never takes a vacation. I bet she's already cooked up something for me.

Mom calls us for dinner. I sit down and see green beans on the table. A stomachache sets in. I expect Mom or Grandpa will say something that will make me want to rip up the rug and crawl through the floor.

On the other hand, Olive's amazingly cool. She and Mom talk about Tucker, and even Grandpa joins in, asking how long her family has lived in Milton, and if she ever bikes on the new reservoir path.

Then, out of nowhere, Olive says, "Rocky, try the green beans. They're great, Ms. Casson."

Is Olive shaming me into eating veggies? If I don't take any, she'll think I'm a fussy baby. That isn't a good look in front of a girl. I slide a few onto my plate, hoping I can choke them down. Mom hands me the ketchup without my asking, but I refuse it. Only little children douse their food with ketchup. I take a bite. They're surprisingly good.

"Not bad," I say. "What's on them?"

Mom's mouth widens into an enormous crater as she processes my question and finally words come out. "Garlic, sesame oil and soy sauce," she says.

I take more. Mom stares at me with pure wonderment as if she saw a magic trick that befuddles her. I hope her heart is strong enough to watch all this vegetable eating.

Olive asks, "Rocky, did you start the science report?"

"Not yet," I answer and stop eating, hardly able to take another bite as she puts the plan in motion.

"This weekend my dad's taking me camping so I can collect specimens of plant and insect life in the Mayflower Mountains. He wants me to get a good grade."

"That's wonderful, Olive," Mom says in the soft voice she gets when a kid mentions their dad.

I can't think about Dad now. I've got to concentrate on my role and get Mom onto the right wavelength about Uncle Bob. I say casual-like, "I used to camp with my dad and my uncle."

"Rocky, are you in that science class too?" Mom asks. If I didn't know better, I'd think Olive has programmed Mom to follow her script, and she's directing Mom to our goal of me going camping.

"I'm not in the same period as Olive, but we have the same assignment." There it is—the big lie hangs in midair like a dark cloud above me.

It's weird when Dad encourages me, SMOOTH, ROCKY.

I ignore him.

"How are you planning to do your project?" Mom asks me.

"Dunno. I guess I'll download images off the Internet."

As Olive predicted, Mom asks, "Is that good enough? Maybe you should go camping too for the report. I could ask Uncle Bob to take you if he's free."

"I don't have to go. It's not a problem."

Everyone drops the camping discussion for the rest of the dinner. Mom and I drive Olive home while Grandpa tackles the dishes. In the car, Olive asks, "Ms. Casson, will you be driving Rocky to the spring dance?"

Holy moly! Where did that come from? Olive never mentioned the dance before. I wasn't gonna tell Mom because she'd make me go. I turn toward the back seat and send eye daggers towards Olive. She smiles at me. She doesn't seem to notice or care I'm mad. The master planner must've been planning this all along. It's her payback for helping me with Max.

"Of course, I'll drive him."

Olive has trapped me. After we drop her off, Mom says, "I'll call Uncle Bob tomorrow to see if we can arrange a camping trip."

"Sure. That's okay with me," I say, trying not to sound too eager.

In my room, I text Olive immediately.

Me: Hey what was that about????

I add a mad emoji face.

Olive: ?

Me: THE DANCE

Olive: FUN!!!!

Me: NOW I HAVE TO GO. Thanks.

I add twenty mad emoji faces.

Dancing. Ugh. This will be torture. I'll make a fool of myself. A year ago, Dad badgered me to learn how to dance because he said girls like a boy with smooth moves. Every Sunday for weeks, he and I practiced the Dab, Nae Nae, Moonwalking, the Twist and others I don't remember from dance DVDs. Mom often stood in the doorway of the living room and observed the silliness. She'd refer to us as the dancing fools.

Then, as suddenly as the dance lessons had begun, they were replaced by Dad lying on the sofa and watching old movies for days. He claimed exhaustion and could hardly do anything, let alone dance.

I bet not-a-ghost dad will be excited to hear I'm going to a real dance. As if on cue, Dad says, ROCKY, THE DANCE WILL BE GREAT. DON'T WHIP YOURSELF INTO A FRENZY. HEY, I WANT TO ASK YOU SOMETHING.

"What?"

DID YOU REALLY ENJOY THE GREEN BEANS TONIGHT OR WERE YOU TRYING TO IMPRESS OLIVE?

"None of your business," I answer.

CHAPTER 16

In Handler's class the next day, Olive informs me she made a deal with Max. This girl is a fast-working dynamo. It would take me forever to know how to even start the negotiations with Max.

"Max wants to go to the dance with us," she says. "I think it's so he won't be like such a loser if he has to go by himself. I agreed to his demand, and in return, he promises not to tell on you."

"Hallelujah," I say. I'll fix my Max problem and be free to return to my main project: cracking the secret. "Going with him to the dance is no prob. Thanks."

"Sure, that's what partners do." Olive shines a smile in my direction that makes my face heat up. I turn my eyes away.

⚽

MOM COMES into my room after work, pushes a couple of sweatshirts off my desk chair and sits down.

"Been running all day. Too many meetings. End of the tax quarter." She stretches out her legs. She's been working harder than ever. I think she wants to keep busy, so she doesn't have to think. It must be tiring to keep such a huge secret hidden.

"I spoke to Uncle Bob," she says, "and he said camping this weekend would be great. He'll pick you up on Friday after school."

"Excellent." At last, she comes through with something I WANT.

"Grandpa will take you to buy hiking boots tomorrow."

As soon as she leaves, I text Olive the news.

Me: camping.

I add a thumbs up emoji.

Olive: it worked!

She adds an amazing gif of fireworks.

Me: buying hiking boots tomorrow

Olive: don't buy anything 2 dorky. Don't want the bears to be shocked you have o fashion sense. send photo from store.

Me: need a copy of the science assignment to make it look official

Olive: Smart. Will make a copy for you.

Me: thanks

Finally, things seem to be falling into place. I have a deal with Max and a plan with Uncle Bob. After this weekend, I will have succeeded in my truth-seeking mission. It's exciting, but also a little scary to enter the unknown.

This camping trip will be so different. The last time we went Dad poured oil inside Uncle Bob's sleeping bag. Uncle Bob returned the prank by adding a ton of hot pepper sauce in the baked beans. I practically busted a gut as Dad ran around the campsite, emptying every water bottle he could lay his hands on to douse the roaring fire in his mouth. The two of them pranked each other all the time.

WHAT A WEEKEND THAT WAS. SO MUCH FUN, Dad says. I MISS

CAMPING WITH YOU BOTH. IT MIGHT BE STRANGE GOING WITHOUT ME.

"It will be," I respond. "Not only will it be strange, it'll be way sad." My nose sniffles, but I'm not getting a cold. I snuff up whatever is trying to leak out.

Dad doesn't respond. He must already know how sad it will be.

FRIDAY, I fly home from school, my feet barely touching the ground. Mom's car is already in the driveway. She'd better not make a big fuss that I'm going away for two days. If she smothers me with kisses or blubbers in front of Uncle Bob, I'm gonna lose it.

I leave my backpack by the door. At 4:00, the doorbell rings, and Mom lets Uncle Bob in. He looks better than the last time I saw him at the funeral when his face was damp and the rims of his eyes were bright red. His hair flops on his forehead like mine and Dad's. I guess all the Casson men have to deal with uncontrollable bangs.

Uncle Bob plants a tiny kiss on Mom's cheek and gives me his usual greeting, squeezing my biceps and saying, "Strong like a prize fighter."

Before I let him utter a word, I announce, "I grew an inch. I play offense instead of goalie. I'm caught up in most of my classes. My bedroom is—"

Mom interrupts my running update. "Bob, it's been a while."

"It has, MB, sorry. Been busy at work and traveling. How's it going in Milton?"

"Better. Rocky has a new friend."

"Made a friend, pal? That's terrific," Uncle Bob says and tosses his arm around me.

"She's a girl," Mom adds. Her eyes have a yucky gleam that makes me want to hurl. Why is this so friggin' cute?

"She's a regular friend, nothing special," I offer in my defense.

Mom continues, "Can you believe that? Growing up."

"Yup. He sure is." Uncle Bob chuckles.

The not-a-ghost dad steps in to rescue me. HEY, ROCKY, Dad says, ASK UNCLE BOB IF HE HAS A GIRLFRIEND. REMEMBER I ALWAYS BUGGED HIM ABOUT GETTING MARRIED AND TOLD HIM HE NEEDED A COUPLE OF LITTLE BOBS OR MAYBE A ROBERTA.

Yeah, like I'm gonna do that.

"Bob, it's times like this..." Mom's voice fades as her words vanish into the air. I could finish her sentence for her. She's missing Dad not being here. "Thanks for doing this," she says.

"I should be thanking you. I can't wait to have some 'quality' time with this guy. It's going to be rad. Did I say that right, Roc?" When grown-ups try to act cool, it comes off silly, but I don't mention it.

Mom says, "Bob, you're a lifesaver. You two haven't been together since..." Again, her face tightens, and she doesn't complete her thought. At least, she isn't crying.

Thankfully, Uncle Bob changes the subject. "I want to say hi to your father before we leave, MB." Mom leads him into the den where Grandpa's sunk in his cushy, red velvet chair with his feet up, reading as usual. I bet he's read almost every book there is. He never stops. He releases the chair's lever to lower the foot rest and stands up to greet Uncle Bob.

A few minutes later, Mom's walking us to the car. I throw my stuffed backpack in. Last night Mom and I had a battle about whether I needed two pairs of boxers and pjs. She insisted I do, but I have no intention of changing my clothes until I'm home on Sunday. Mom is living on another planet if she thinks I need so much stuff to go camping. When I went with Dad, she was never involved in the packing and didn't know what we brought.

Mom gives me a hug but refrains from slobbering on me. She says she'll miss me and to have fun.

Well, I might have some fun this weekend, but I'm laser-focused on my mission. A few bugs and plants will NOT sidetrack me. By Sunday I will have blasted her secret into molecules of dust.

⚽

OUR CAMPSITE IS deep in the woods. I breathe in the fresh pine smell in the air, which is way superior compared to having to inhale those chemicals they use to prevent schools from becoming a wasteland. From this spot, you can sometimes glimpse the tall buildings of Boston on a clear day, but now it's too cloudy. Dad and Uncle Bob always chose the remotest sites where they could fool around without other campers nearby.

When we finish setting up the tent, Uncle Bob proposes a short hike before dinner to make a dent on the list of things I'm supposed to gather for my "fake" science report. Uncle Bob unpacks a bunch of jars, a net and baggies for the specimens.

"I predict great success," he announces, ever the optimist. Dad referred to him as my *funcle* because he was upbeat, unlike Dad whose moods could be unpredictable.

The path is bumpy with roots jutting out ready to trip us. So far, no blisters from my new boots. I gather some pinecones and leaves that aren't all brown and shriveled from the winter. Later, I'll research what they are on the computer. For a second, I forget I don't have a real assignment. Maybe I could do a report for extra credit, and then I wouldn't be a total liar, only half a liar.

I'm anxious to question Uncle Bob, but Olive advised me to wait until tomorrow and catch him off guard, so he doesn't figure out the camping trip was a con job. I'll bring up the subject of how Dad died as if it just occurred to me.

Uncle Bob calls from up ahead, "Hey, Rocky, don't pick any plants with three leaves. I don't want you all rashed up when I take you home. Your mom will kill me."

"Ha. Ha. Very funny." Dad taught me how to identify poison ivy and made me promise never to eat berries in the woods. He didn't have to warn me about mushrooms because I'd NEVER put one of those things in my mouth.

I step over a fallen branch and notice a rather large black beetle sitting perfectly still; he could be dead. I scoop him up and shove him into a plastic bag. Once captured, his legs shoot out in rapid fire. Poor guy searches for an escape. Maybe I should let him go, but instead, I make a few little slits in the bag so he can breathe. The fresh air calms him down.

Uncle Bob shout-whispers something that sounds like "playing Santas." Dad and he had lots of silly jokes, and this may be one of them. I'm not getting fooled into imagining he sees little fat men with white beards in red suits throwing a ball or messing around.

I catch up to him. He points to a green bug on an old tree stump and whispers, "Praying mantis."

The creature has small, funny front legs that bend in two places and back legs similar to a grasshopper. His triangle-shaped head has bulgy eyes spread so far apart it's a miracle he can focus on anything. I've never been up close with a bug like that before. Uncle Bob traps him in the net and nudges him into a jar.

"Enough for today," he says after his conquest. "We'll find a whole lot more tomorrow. Let's go back, make a fire and have dinner."

While we're eating, Uncle Bob reminisces. "Your dad got me that time he shut off the hot water in the showers at the state park in the Berkshires. I froze my buns off."

"Yeah." I laugh, recalling Uncle Bob shivering with only a little towel wrapped around his middle. Dad stole his clothes too.

"And you put a bunch of earthworms in Dad's jacket pockets," I remind him.

"So I did," he says, with great pride. "Never let a big brother get the best of you. That's my motto." It's nice to talk about Dad without all the usual overpowering sadness.

This IS fun. Tomorrow will be heavy when we get into the serious stuff.

Dad says, I HOPE THE TRUTH ISN'T WORSE THAN YOU ANTICIPATE.

CHAPTER 11

At the first hint of daybreak, I wake up listening to the birds outside the tent squawk at the top of their lungs while they search for breakfast. Woods' noises used to give me the shivers, but Dad devised a plan to cure me of my fears.

He'd get me up in the middle of the night to go hiking. We wore headlamps and carried enormous flashlights. Along the way, he'd tell stories that cracked me up. Whenever there was a strange rustling sound or the call of some nocturnal animal, we'd stop and discuss if we were scared and should run back to the tent, or if they were normal sounds of the woods and not dangerous.

Today, there's an early morning icy chill in the air because we're so high up on the mountain. I hate to leave my toasty sleeping bag to brave the cold, but nature calls. Uncle Bob's grinning in his sleep. Must be some happy dreaming going on.

I zip open the tent quietly and slip out to pee.

By the time I return, Uncle Bob's gone. I assume he left for the same reason. No need for me to change clothes because I'm wearing what I slept in. I grab my toothbrush, toothpaste and a bottle of water and head outside. I always do a minimum of washing up when we camp. I'm not that much of a savage.

Uncle Bob isn't back when I return. I'm not worried until I hear a croaking noise echoing from beyond a clump of trees. I listen, trying to figure out what kind of animal could be making that noise.

Then I hear: "Ro...ock...ee." That can only be Uncle Bob. No one else knows my name out here. He could be setting me up for a major prank. Dad's not here, so I'm probably his new prankee. I decide not to play along with whatever he's cooked up and be cool and ignore him.

Then a scream rings out through the woods. "He...elp!"

This is no joke. In all their mischief-making, Uncle Bob and Dad would never shout that word without a good reason. I take off toward the sound. In a clearing, past the trees, a man lies on the ground. He doesn't much resemble Uncle Bob; I approach him cautiously. There are raised, angry blotches covering his face, and his lips are ten times their normal size. His left eye is swollen shut and his neck and arms are red. If this scene was in a graphic novel, there'd be bolts of pain shooting out of him.

"Ne...est," Uncle Bob grunts.

"What happened?" I ask, keeping my distance and staring in astonishment at his hideous transformation. I'm not sure he'll be able to get up on his own. I wish there was another adult here to take charge of this, but it's all on me.

"Bites," he says.

"Can you stand?' I ask.

"Think so." His other eye slowly closing.

"I'll help you." I hook my arm around his shoulder and under his armpit and pull. He doesn't move. I'm not strong enough to lift him on my own.

"You've got to try too." I urge him. "On the count of three," I instruct, "One, two, three, up."

He's on his feet, but with his eyes barely slits, he stumbles around. I take his hand and lead him toward the tent. When we're almost there, he pulls away, leans over to the side and barfs up the undigested remains of last night's dinner.

Dad says, THIS IS TERRIBLE! HE MUST BE HAVING AN ALLERGIC REACTION. HELP HIM.

I know. I know. But what am I supposed to do? I need help! I shout at Dad in my head.

Once we're inside the tent, I say to Uncle Bob, "I never knew you're allergic to bees."

"Not. Wasn't. Didn't know," he groans, pointing to his backpack. "Kit."

I take out the first aid kit and open it. I unzip a side compartment which is loaded with prescription bottles. They all have long, hard-to-pronounce medicine names and are for Ronald Owen Casson. I don't remember Dad taking lots of pills, and now I can't ask Uncle Bob what they're for. I return them and look for medicine for Uncle Bob.

"What...is...in...there?" He struggles to form each word.

I read off the non-prescription items. "Band-Aids, bacitracin, aspirin, Benadryl, and—"

Uncle Bob interrupts, "Two bened..." His voice trails off as if he ran out of steam, but it must be the Benedryl.

I give him two pills with some water. He has difficulty swallowing with his too big tongue, but gets them down.

Now what am I supposed to do? Being out of cell range is another huge complication. Usually, I don't mind ditching the distractions of being connected, but now it means I'll have to search the woods all by myself for other campers. I doubt many people are on the mountain in this cool weather.

A loud "NO" bangs in my eardrums. Do not go anywhere on your own. You might get lost. The not-a-ghost dad is stern.

I have no choice. I argue.

You have to get him to the ranger's station, Dad says.

Uncle Bob's in no condition to drive.

You should drive, he says.

Have you lost your mind? Me?

You can do it. I taught you.

Some Sunday mornings when Mom slept late, Dad took me to a deserted parking lot and taught me how to drive. I learned to do figure eights around trashcans and back up in a straight line. Mom would have blown her top if she knew what we were up to. Dad must understand driving in an empty parking lot and on a mountain road are polar opposites.

I can't do this, I say, trying to get him to see reason. But if something bad happens to Uncle Bob because I was too chicken, I'll never forgive myself.

"Uncle Bob, I'll drive you to the ranger's station," I say, crossing my fingers he'll say no.

He doesn't. I'm not sure Uncle Bob even understands what I'm saying, but he pulls on my arm for leverage and struggles to sit up, grimacing in pain.

"Keys...in...my...jacket."

I guess he does agree to this insane plan. I fish through his pockets and find the car keys. "Got them." They jangle in my shaky hands, so I clench my fists until my knuckles are bright white.

"Are you sure there isn't another way?" I ask Uncle Bob, desperately hoping he'll come up with a safer plan.

"I'm sure." Uncle Bob and not-a-ghost dad answer me at the same time.

I guide Uncle Bob as he hobbles to the car. I open the passenger's door for him, but he says, "Backseat."

OMG, he isn't even planning to sit beside me and tell me what to do. Uncle Bob crawls in the backseat and lies down. I can't put the seat belt on him in that position.

I get behind the wheel, check out the controls and fumble around with my foot for the gas and brake pedals. Breathing in and out a few times to steady my nerves, I turn the key. A screeching sound assaults my ears, because I turned the key too far. I emit a long exhale to center myself and try again. Perfect this time; the engine hums.

I move my foot to the gas with one thought: *I hope I don't kill us both.*

CHAPTER 18

Releasing the shift lever into Drive, I press on the gas, but the car doesn't move.

"I can't do this," I whine, filled with frustration and fright.

You CAN DO IT, ROCKY, Dad reassures me. He's pretending this is another Sunday outing, but this isn't even close to normal.

Dad continues, IF YOU RELAX, IT'LL GO BETTER. TRUST YOURSELF. YOU'RE A GOOD DRIVER. REMEMBER WHAT I TAUGHT YOU. I WISH I WERE THERE TO HELP YOU.

"Me, too," I answer, speaking in a normal voice because Uncle Bob is too out of it to be aware I'm talking to myself. I close my eyes and picture I'm high above this scene, floating on a cloud. I imagine Dad beside me, flashing a smile and a wink, showing his complete confidence in my ability. I shake myself back into reality and tumble off the cloud, falling into the driver's seat.

I examine the dashboard again. This time, I see the red light indicating the parking brake is on. What a dummy. I bet I'm gonna forget a ton of stuff. I press the brake release and move my foot to the gas. This time, I overcompensate with too much pressure. We zoom forward.

Without thinking, my left foot darts for the brake pedal. We stop with a wallop. I barely miss bumping my head on the steering wheel.

Uncle Bob moans, "Easy, buddy."

The car may not be moving, but the boiling blood in my veins races around my body in overdrive. This could be heart attack territory.

You're fine. Slow breathing, Dad encourages me.

This time, I bear down on the gas pedal gently as if it might crumble with too much force. We inch along. At this speed, it could take an hour to get to the ranger's station, so I give it more gas. The speedometer rises to 25. I try to hold that speed as I navigate this narrow and twisty mountain road.

There's a sudden sharp curve to the left which I maneuver okay, but as I'm re-centering the car into the middle of the road, a frantic honking shatters the air. Another car is almost on top of me. It won't have room to pass. I turn the wheel to get out of the way, but too far. Our car drifts down a slight embankment as I slam on the brakes. We stop inches from a tree.

Every moveable part of me quivers like a mass of Jell-O. I lean over the seat to check on Uncle Bob.

"Oh...oh." He chokes when he tries to speak. At least I didn't kill him or me. There's a familiar wetness in his voice. Mom made that same sound in the weeks after Dad died, when she was constantly sucking back tears.

"I told you I couldn't do this," I cry to Dad and get out of the car to survey the situation. A loud yelling rolls down from the road. The car I almost hit is parked, and a man marches toward us, shouting as if he's gonna kill someone. Road rage. If he's carrying a weapon, we're sitting ducks. I dash into the car and lock the doors a split second before an extremely tall, thin man with a shaved head raps on my window.

"Were you sleeping while you were driving? You are completely reckless. You could've killed us. I have my young daughter with me. Are you an idiot?"

"Sorry, sir," I say through my closed window, unsure whether he can hear me.

The guy gets quiet and gives me the once-over. "Hey," he says, "You're a kid. How old are you? What are you doing driving a car? Did you steal it? Is this your idea of a joyride? I'm going to the ranger's station to call the cops."

"The cops!" I shout.

"Open it," he commands, making a circular motion with his hand in case I don't understand what he means. I open the window partway but keep my finger on the button in case I have to raise it in a hurry.

I stammer, "Uh. My uncle...backseat...sick." My jitters prevent me from constructing a complete sentence. I sense my heart rising into my throat. I close my mouth before it jumps out and tries to escape from this disaster.

The man's eyes move toward the backseat. "What's the matter with him?"

I inhale a couple of times to grab enough air to speak. "He's full of bee stings. He can't see or walk. He needs a doctor."

"No more driving for you, kid. We'll take you. Open the door."

Should I? This is a time you would probably wish you weren't responsible for making the decision. The man seems okay, and he IS a father. He wouldn't murder us in front of his own daughter, would he?

He helps Uncle Bob out, grabbing him around the waist to guide him to the road. I review the pros and cons of breaking one of Mom's holiest rules: not to go with a stranger. If I do this, I'll pay a heavy price when Mom finds out. But I shouldn't have to, because this whole fiasco is her fault. If she had told me the truth from the beginning, Uncle Bob wouldn't be sick, and I wouldn't be dealing with this very angry stranger.

The man settles Uncle Bob in the backseat. I slide in next to him and fasten his seatbelt and then my own. Straight ahead of me in the front seat, a girl's brownish-reddish pony tail rises above the headrest. Either this is a gosh darn coincidence, or perhaps I'm still curled up in my sleeping bag immersed in a fantastic dream, and this isn't happening in real time.

Rattled, I ask, "Olive, is that you?"

There's no answer. The father gets in the car, reaches out to pull off the girl's headphones and motions to me. "Do you recognize this kid?"

She turns toward the back, and for once, Olive has no words.

"How do you know my daughter?"

I answer, "School."

"You live in Milton?"

"Yup."

"I never saw you before."

"I'm kind of new."

Olive's eyes bulge out of their sockets until they almost touch mine. She's startled as if she's seen a ghost, but it's only me.

CHAPTER 19

O live does a giraffe neck-stretch until her head is practically in the backseat. She mouths, "What happened?"

I reply, "Allergic reaction."

She studies my uncle, whose face is ghastly and enormous, not his usual handsome self.

Dad used to kid him about being good-looking. "So, Bob," he'd say, "where are the girls now, Mr. Popular?" Uncle Bob's face would always redden when Dad teased him.

Olive again formulates her words without sound and asks, "Did you get the answer?"

I shake my head no.

"Rats." That word she belts out loud and clear.

Her dad says, "Don't be upset, honey, there will be plenty of time to collect lots of specimens after we get your friend's uncle help." He assumed the "rats" comment was because she's disappointed she might miss their camping trip.

If I know Olive, she'll be eager to seize on this mishap to scuttle her outdoor adventure. She proves me right immediately when she tells her clueless dad, "We don't have to still go. I can print images from the computer. It'll be fine. We can go home."

"Oh, no, sweetheart, we're going. I'd never miss a chance to soak up some nature with you."

Olive turns toward me, and her eyes and mouth pinch into a knot like she sucked on a whole lemon.

We pull into the ranger's station. Her father instructs us to wait while he makes the arrangements. When her dad is out of the car, Olive whispers, "Can you ask your uncle now?"

"Are you kidding? He's way too sick," I also keep my voice low, but honestly, I doubt Uncle Bob's following any of this.

"So, this whole camping plan was a giant fiasco," she says. Her dad returns and looks glum. The ranger is away and left a note that he's checking on some campers who ran into trouble. He'll be back around 10:00.

Olive's dad says, "We shouldn't wait. Your uncle's having a severe reaction. I'm driving you to the hospital. It'll be faster than calling for an ambulance."

"Thank you," I say, grateful there's an adult in charge, and I'm off the hook.

Olive's dad says, "When we're at the bottom of the mountain and have cell service, you can call your parents and tell them to meet us at Quincy Hospital."

"Parent," Olive corrects him. Me, I would have ignored that.

"What?" her dad asks.

Olive explains, "He only has one parent. A mom. No dad."

"Oh, sorry." He gets quiet. This is the typical response when a person gets that upsetting information. It's awkward for everyone.

When we leave the mountain road, the dad reaches back and hands me his phone. I know Mom won't recognize the number and might think this is a crank call, so the second she says hello, I tell her it's me and not to hang up.

"Rocky!" She sounds like I scared the bejeezus out of her. Then she unleashes a boatload of questions. "Rocky, why are you calling from a strange number? Are you okay? What happened? Something bad happened. Where's Bob? Whose phone is this? Where are you?"

"Take a breath, Mom, I'm okay. I'm with Olive and her dad. Uncle Bob had a bad reaction to some bees or something. We're going to Quincy Hospital." I do not mention my driving, which would only produce hysterics.

"Are you sure you're okay?" she asks again.

"I'm sure. Meet us at the hospital."

"I'm leaving immediately."

Mom hangs up, and I pass the phone back. "She'll be there as soon as she can."

"Good," Olive's dad says.

For the rest of the drive, only Uncle Bob's soft yowls and occasional sniffles break the silence. When we arrive at the emergency center, Olive's dad rushes in and comes out with two guys and a stretcher. They want the patient's name and ID. I give them his full name and explain I didn't bring his wallet, so no ID. I think they're required to take care of him anyway. They wheel him in. The rest of us trail along behind until we're told we can't go farther.

Olive's dad says, "We'll stay with you until your mom comes."

"That's not necessary," I say, "I'm fine. You don't have to. I don't want you to miss more of your camping trip."

Olive scowls at me.

"No arguments. We're staying." Her dad buys us hot chocolate from a vending machine, and the three of us sit to wait.

The last time I was in a hospital was that horrendous Sunday evening. I remember walking in, confident everything would be okay. Doctors can fix lots of things, especially for a strong and healthy guy like my dad, or so I thought. It never crossed my mind for a second, he might be dead. No one in my class had a parent who died. Some had parents who lived in another city because of divorce, but they were alive.

Reliving the most horrible day of my life ends when Mom bursts into the waiting room as if she was shot out of a cannon aimed directly at us. First, she grabs me and hugs me, covering my face with kisses, which is humiliating in front of Olive.

I pull away and say, "I'm fine. Mom. Really, I am."

She studies me and nods her head up and down in agreement. Olive's dad introduces himself and tells her what happened. When he mentions my driving, Mom's eyes narrow and pierce into my core, a sure sign a major league punishment will be coming.

YOU CAN'T BLAME HER FOR BEING UPSET ABOUT YOUR DRIVING. SHE'S BEING CAUTIOUS, the not-a-ghost dad says after a long silence. He's quick to rush into my head to defend Mom.

He's right of course. I would have been shocked if she was okay with that.

Olive's dad offers to gather up our gear at the campsite and arrange to get Uncle Bob's car down from the mountain.

"I'm so grateful to you," Mom says, "What a wonderful coincidence you happened by when you did. Thank you." She shakes his hand and gives Olive a hug, which Olive seems okay with, so I am too.

"Nice to meet you, Rocky," Olive's dad says and pats my shoulder. "Hope your uncle is better soon."

"Thank you, Mr. Jordan. Can you please bring my specimens with you? I've got a beetle and a praying mantis I want to keep. Also, I need my backpack. It's the denim one."

"Sure thing," he says.

After they're gone, Mom leaves me in the waiting room to check in with the doctors. I sag into my seat, wiped out. I glance at the other people around me. Some are smiling and chatting, not anticipating bad news. Others study their hands, which are in constant motion, or they gaze up at the ceiling as if the cracks are fascinating. They're the ones who are lost in their own heads, afraid of what's coming.

Things can go very, very wrong in a place like this.

CHAPTER 20

I'm antsy from my head to my butt sitting in this hard chair in the hospital waiting room. I walk around a little to shake off the feeling, checking the time on my phone repeatedly. This is a bad sign that she's been gone so long. My heart-elevator rides to the bottom floor.

I park myself in a more cushiony seat. "Please not Uncle Bob, too," I pray in an almost silent whisper and pull my feet onto the chair, burying my head on my knees. Each time the automatic doors whoosh open and it's not Mom, I get a little sadder. I want to get out of this hospital. I hate it here.

Finally, it's Mom. Her eyes are bright and clear, and her lips lift at the ends when she sees me. Dad used to say, "MB, I bet no other accountant in the world has such a pretty smile. Rocky's lucky he has that same magic." That was always my cue to make a quick exit before their sappiness dripped all over me. They'd tease how they could get rid of me fast when they wanted to clear the room.

The not-a-ghost dad must see what I do, because his voice gives off happy vibes as he says, SEE, UNCLE BOB'S GOING TO BE FINE.

Mom reports, "The doctors are giving Uncle Bob medicine to fight the reaction, IV antibiotics and fluids. They found a few dead hornets under his shirt. That species is known for stinging repeatedly when their nest is disturbed. From now on, Uncle Bob will have to carry medicine with him whenever he goes into the woods in case he runs into a swarm of those killer hornets again. He's responding well, and a friend of his will pick him up later. We can leave now."

So today, for us, the news in this hospital is good. That is, if Mom can be trusted—which she cannot be. She has lied before and might be doing it again.

"Can I see him?" I ask, which is what I should have demanded that terrible Sunday, but I was in shock and not thinking straight.

"No, he's sleeping," Mom answers.

Oh, oh. My suspicious antennae rise until they wave in the air fully extended. What if Mom's up to her usual tricks and protecting me from some real bad news? Dad would complain she babied me too much, and then she'd complain back that Dad took too many risks with me. I bet the driving lessons would fall into that category.

This time, I'm standing my ground, which I should've done when Dad died. I'm not letting her shove me out of here before I'm ready.

"I have to see him, or I'm not going with you," I insist in a booming voice which interrupts people's quiet thoughts about their own problems. The commotion causes them to glance toward us.

Mom's eyes double their normal size as if she received an electric shock. She's not used to me being this forceful. "But he's fine. I just told you," she says.

"How do I know? Sometimes you keep secrets because you want to protect me. I'm not a little kid anymore. I'm almost a full-fledged teenager."

"But I told you the truth." She defends herself.

"Maybe this time. But you don't all the time."

"All parents protect their children."

Boy, she'd never let me get away with such a cop-out. I can hear her scolding, "So, would doing blah blah be okay because everyone else is doing that?"

"Dad told you not to baby me." I'm not easing up on her.

She continued, "He wasn't perfect, you know. I'll take you into Uncle Bob's room to prove I'm telling the truth. Will you be satisfied then?"

"Yes." I jam my angry hands into my pockets and follow her down the hallway. When we push open the door to Uncle Bob's room, I see lots of plastic bags sending liquid into him and a monitor flashing numbers. So much medical stuff is scary, even if it's helping him.

Uncle Bob's eyes are closed. Most likely, he's sleeping, but then again, I'm not in a trusting mood. I poke him on his arm but get no response.

Mom says, "Rocky, there's no need to wake him. Let him be. They gave him medicine to help him sleep so he wouldn't be in pain."

I poke him again, much harder.

"Yowie!" he yelps and opens his eyes. "What the heck?"

"It's me," I say, "Are you okay?"

"Yeah. Thanks, Rocky. If it wasn't for you... You're my hero."

Mom beams. She may be mad about the driving, but she's a tiny bit proud of me at the same time.

"No prob," I say. He takes my hand and squeezes it. I give him a little squeeze back.

"Raincheck on the camping, buddy."

I lean in close as if I'm gonna kiss him on the cheek and whisper in his ear, "I had some questions for you, but I never got a chance to ask them."

"Sorry. I'm too fuzzy now from the meds."

"Can you call me?"

"I'm off to Japan as soon as the doctor gives me permission to travel. With the time difference and all the work ahead of me, it'll have to wait. I'll bring you something special from there. How would you like a sumo wrestler's outfit?"

"Ha. Ha. Never gonna wear that and let my butt hang out for the world to see."

"I want you to believe me, Rocky, this is a real business trip."

What does he mean "a real business trip?" Are there fake ones? The only thing I know is that Dad hated his business trips. Sometimes he'd argue with Mom about whether he had to go.

He'd complain that those brokers' regional meetings were like being in jail. He never discussed where he went, as if he was working undercover, keeping the whole trip hush hush. When he came home, it always took him a few days to bounce back to his old self. But I never thought those trips weren't real. More questions for Uncle Bob.

"It can wait, Uncle Bob. See you when you get back."

ON THE WAY HOME, Mom says, "I can't believe you thought it was okay for you to drive Uncle Bob to the hospital! That was dangerous."

"It was lucky Dad taught me how to drive." I had already described our Sunday morning lessons to her. "I had no choice," I defend myself, "There are times you have to take a chance."

"You sound like Dad. Promise me you'll never do anything so foolish again."

"I won't promise. It was up to me to save Uncle Bob."

"I know you were concerned and wanted to help Uncle Bob, and I'm grateful how things turned out this time. But no more driving until you get your license, or there will be a serious punishment. Take this as your warning." Her tone leaves no doubt she's furious with me, but I don't care. Things didn't go how I wanted either.

"Will you be able to finish the report?" Mom is concerned about my phony assignment.

"Yeah. I'll use the Internet." Lying to her is crummy, but I guess that makes us more alike now. We both have our secrets.

"I'll call Olive's parents on Monday and thank them again."

Knowing what Mom is like, I say, "Do NOT make any arrangements for family get-togethers. Please." This is just the type of plan Mom would think is fabulous.

"It might be fun."

"No, it wouldn't be." I need to bat that idea into another galaxy.

She persists, "We used to get together with Shawn and his family for dinner, and you never objected to that."

"This is different."

After a few minutes, a goofy grin appears on her face, and she says, "Understood."

"Good." A bunch of adults around the dinner table gawking at Olive and me would be more disastrous than Max's snitching to Ms. Malone.

AT HOME, I shower and lie on my bed, stoked with anger. Maybe I'm destined to never know the truth.

Dad says, SORRY THINGS DIDN'T WORK OUT THE WAY YOU WANTED. BUT SUPER GLAD UNCLE BOB'S OKAY. I LOVE THAT GUY.

"Me too. Duh."

ALL THAT GOOD PLANNING RUINED BY HORNETS.

"Dad, I'm begging you to tell me what happened."

I WISH I COULD.

"You're a lost cause. I'm giving up."

MY NUMBER ONE SON DOES NOT GIVE UP.

"Dad, you of all people should understand that sometimes you run out of options, like you did when you died. All your options were finished, kaput, cancelled, ended, terminated, over." The words *wrecked, shattered, ruined, destroyed*...pour out of me.

My rant halts with the ping of an incoming text.

Shawn: Hey, man. My birthday party Friday. BLAST!!!!!!!

Me: Can't come. school dance

Shawn: Ditch that

Me: Promised a friend

Shawn: Who?

Me: Olive

Shawn: A girl?????? Ditch girlfriend. I'm your best friend.

Me: NOT a girlfriend

Shawn: Are you sure - chuckle chuckle?

Shawn sends an emoji with its tongue hanging out.

Me: she suckered me into going

Shawn: sympathy

Me: Yeah. Right.

Shawn: MAJOR BUMMER.

Me: DOUBLE MAJOR COLOSSAL BUMMER.

Shawn: Come back to Whitman.

Me: I'm stuck here forever. Any news from your mom?

Shawn: Nope.

I never thought Shawn would come up with anything, but I had to give it a try. Now that attempt will join the others in the ever-growing column of failures. If the secret swallows me, I could be digested in its belly acid, bit by bit, until there's nothing left of me.

"Dad, even if I could figure out how to get to Whitman, what am I supposed to do there? You never told me."

No answer. The not-a-ghost dad always dodges the tough questions. When I need him the most, he isn't here.

CHAPTER 21

M ondays are tough, but this one makes my head hurt. I thought I was gonna wake up today with the mystery gone, but I'm no closer to the truth than I was before the hornet fiasco. Desperate for a day off, I stay in bed and wait for Mom to realize I'm MIA.

Sure enough, in a few minutes, there's a knock. I grunt, "Come in."

"Are you sick?" she asks and brushes her lips on my forehead in that fake temperature-taking, which is a lame-o excuse to sneak in a kiss.

"My stomach. Might throw up," I reply.

"You'd better stay home then, close to the bathroom. I have a big meeting today I can't miss, but Grandpa's here if you need anything.

I'll check in later." Living with Grandpa makes it easier for Mom to be away, but I'm used to staying by myself since I turned twelve.

"Uh...uh." I clutch my middle for a dose of realism, in case she worries I'm sliding into the same routine like after Dad died when I needed lots of "sick" days. But today is a one-off, at least I'm telling myself that.

After she leaves, I go back to sleep. Next thing I know it's ten o'clock. I drag myself out of bed.

As I pass by Mom's room, the not-a-ghost dad asks, DID YOU EVER THINK OF LOOKING IN THERE FOR A CLUE?

It's amazing how I have the same idea, at the same time. Our minds work alike, maybe 'cause we're father and son.

As I cross the threshold into Mom's room, another of Dad's favorite routines comes to mind. He'd say, "Hippo...hippo...hippo..." And stop as if he couldn't remember how to end the word. Then I'd call out, "Hippopotamus."

"No," he'd say with great glee, "Hippo-crite."

We'd both laugh. It wasn't until sixth grade I understood what the word meant after a unit on the presidential election. Today, I'm the hypocrite going into Mom's room without permission because I don't give her those same rights.

I pause by the photos on Mom's dresser. There's me on Dad's shoulders when I was six or seven and another of Mom holding me when I was a baby. She also framed the absolute most embarrassing photo of me ever from fourth grade. That year, I had enormous grown-up front teeth that overpowered my mouth making me look like a doofus. I'm thankful I grew into those monstrosities.

I open and close some drawers like detectives do on crime shows, but I have no idea what I'm hoping to find. I guess I'll know it when I see it. Next, I check her desk. There's a stack of cards from people who wrote sympathy about Dad, side-by-side with the thank you notes she writes to people who said sorry at the funeral or at our house. It's beyond me why people need a thank you for that. It's not like they brought us a present or anything.

Underneath the cards, a sheet of paper sticks out with the name of a hospital. I pull it out and read:

Dear Ms. Casson,

Please accept our condolences to you and your son, Ronald Junior, on the loss of your husband. We know this must have been a terrible shock for you. We want you to know we did all we could to provide Ronald with the very best of care whenever he was in our facility. If you have any questions, please don't hesitate to contact Dr. Frank Sandler, who was in charge of his care here.

Sincerely yours,
Samuel Good, MD
Director
Kenmore Hospital

Dad was in the hospital! And more than once! I never knew. He only went away for business.

Was Dad's heart so bad he had to be hospitalized? And why would they keep that a secret? Why not tell me he had heart trouble? Did he have an operation they were hiding? My questions form at such a furious rate they overflow my brain. I look down as if I expect to see a mound of them on the floor waiting for someone to clean them up. This letter is definite proof Mom's been lying to me.

I pull out my phone to take a picture of the letter, but my legs are boneless. I wait a minute to stabilize myself so the photo won't come out blurry. When I'm steady, I snap it and return the letter to where I found it.

What kind of a family keeps a secret like this?

CHAPTER 22

Back in my room, I fling myself onto the bed with enough force to make a permanent body-shaped dent in the mattress. Luckily, the bed doesn't collapse. I press the home button to bring my phone back to life to reread the letter.

As the screen lights up, the door opens. I shove the phone under the pillow when Grandpa, who doesn't subscribe to the knocking-first privacy rule, walks in.

"How are you feeling? You look like a ghost," he says.

Ordinarily, that line would crack me up. My dad's dead, and he is not a ghost. I'm alive and look like one, but today nothing is funny.

Earlier I pretended to be sick, but now I'm really miserable. There's a shooting pain splitting my head with each side punching the other to win the-who-hurts-the-most prize.

"How about eating something?" Grandpa asks.

"Grandpa, did you visit my dad when he was in the hospital?"

"No."

"But you do know he was there."

"I don't exactly remember. Talk to your mother." He must be under strict orders not to divulge a thing. He's part of the conspiracy too.

"Grandpa, did my dad mention his heart sickness to you?"

"He didn't discuss his health. Come eat a little. You'll feel better."

"Soon."

He leaves, probably relieved to make his exit before I ask another forbidden question.

I can't understand why they'd hide Dad's being in the hospital. Everyone knows someone who was in the hospital, and it's never a big deal or a big secret. Once, Shawn's mother was in the hospital—I forget what for—but Shawny visited her. He said the hospital food was way worse than Whitman Middle, which was difficult to believe. Another kid in my class had a grandmother in an old people's hospital for a long time. I'm not sure if he visited her, but he came over for lots of playdates because his mom was always there.

I go downstairs. Grandpa suggests tomato or chicken soup. I pick tomato and mention I could eat a grilled cheese. He moves into action.

"Grandpa, how come you stayed in this big house by yourself and never moved?"

"I'm used to it," he answers, as he puts a bowl in front of me. "I'm not so good with change."

"Me either." I throw some croutons into the soup. Grandpa brings me the sandwich and rests his arm around my shoulder, leaving it there for a long time.

Maybe I inherited the not-being-good-with-change gene from him. I can visualize my old house in my old neighborhood as if it has been tattooed on my brain.

Grandpa joins me at the table and says, "You've had a lot of changes. I'm sorry about the difficulties you've had to face."

Me too.

I'D BET a million dollars Olive will text me the minute school ends. I plan to show her the letter. She'll know what I should do.

At precisely 3:00, my phone pings.

Olive: Where were you????

Me: Home

Olive: Sick????

Me: maybe

Olive: Really?

Me: No. day off.

Olive: O

I send a sad emoji

Olive: ?

Me: Can't talk now

Olive: Are you practicing your dance moves?

Me: Maybe I won't go.

Olive: YOU HAVE TO! You have a deal with Max. What are you wearing????

I don't reply.

Olive: SERIOUSLY YOU HAVE TO LOOK RIGHT!!!! jeans and a button-down and COOL shoes

I don't reply.

Olive: What's up with you????

Me: Bad day. Explain tomorrow.

I wish I hadn't agreed to go to the dance, but I have to keep Max's trap shut. It's like there's a championship ping pong game underway inside my head. I'm playing both sides of the net and still losing.

A short time later, Mom comes up. She's home earlier than usual.

The first thing she does is recheck my forehead. She's glad I ate. I pass along Olive's clothing instructions for Friday night.

"We'll go to the mall tomorrow if you're better. The dance will be so much fun."

Mom's ridiculously giddy I'm going. She doesn't deserve to be off the hook and think I've adjusted to this disastrous move and the new school. I'm going to puncture her bubble.

"I'm going, but not because I want to. No need for you to get so happy."

My bitter tone succeeds in changing her expression. For a moment I regret my harshness, but I'm still angry at her. I don't think I'll ever forgive her.

You should apologize, Dad says.

The hospital. You guys didn't tell me. I'm so freaking mad.

Mom and I agreed to that, he explains.

Well, I figured that out by myself, but doesn't your agreement die when you die? Why were you there?

I can't tell you. Talk to the doctor.

How will I do that?

I don't know yet.

I can't count on him for anything.

CHAPTER 23

The next day at lunch Olive empties her cooler bag and displays her normal, brought-from-home lunch, which makes me jealous. She demands I start talking. I procrastinate, parting the food on my plate to make a path and then mush it back together, watching the pieces of chipped beef drown in gravy waves. It's pretty disgusting.

Before I show her the letter, I ask her once more, "Will Max stick to the arrangement after the dance?"

"Max will be fine," she says, "and you've got a bad habit of avoiding certain questions. What happened yesterday?"

Olive can be relentless. You dodge her at your peril. If she doesn't go into "word" work, she should be a prison guard. There'd be no escapees. She's the most alert person I ever met.

I'm trapped, so here goes. "I found a letter about my dad."

"And?"

"He was in the hospital, and I never knew."

"How did they manage to keep that a secret?"

"I have an idea, but I'm not sure."

"Secrets. Bah," Olive says. "My parents could get caught in their lie that Michael is in college. What happens when he comes home? People will ask him where he goes to school. What is he supposed to say? Did they even make a plan for that?" Her eyes drop as if suddenly she has to memorize something on the tabletop. "Unless they know he's not ever coming home!" she gasps. "Oh no!" Her hands rush up and cover her face.

What do I do if she cries?

"Of course, he'll come home," I say calmly.

She lowers her hands. I reach out and pat one of them, aware I've never touched her before. A strange sensation runs from my fingertips to my brain. I pull my hand back. She smiles at me, so I guess it was okay.

You're crushing on her. My not-a-ghost dad seems compelled to make an obnoxious comment.

Double, triple, quadruple ugh.

I'M SO NOT DISCUSSING OLIVE WITH YOU. I hope he hears me shouting inside my head.

Olive asks, "Were you snooping yesterday?"

"Um...yeah." I pass my phone to her so she can read the letter.

"Wow, Rocky, that's heavy duty. Are you okay?"

"No. I want to call the doctor to find out why my dad was there."

"You can't call." She's emphatic. "You won't pass for an adult. No way. They won't give you any information, and they will, for sure, call your mother."

"I could disguise my voice."

"Try it on me. Pretend I'm the hospital person, and you're an old man like your grandfather."

I swallow the last bit of my vanilla pudding, the only passable food in school, and stare at my feet, imagining my voice originating from down there. I clear my throat to create an old man's croak and say, "I want to speak with the doctor. My name is—"

Olive cuts me off. "No way you can pull that off. Sorry."

"I want a do-over. Give me a sec." For my next effort, I close my eyes so Olive doesn't distract me.

"Hello," I say in a voice so deep it hurts to talk. I'm gonna have the worst sore throat ever. I continue, "Doctor, my name is Ronald Casson. My father was your patient and—"

"Won't work."

"Nuts." If this was a year from now, my voice would be lower, and I could pass for a grown man. Maybe Amazon sells voice changers for people in the witness protection program. I wonder how much they cost.

"Rocky, did you ever stop to think your mom may have a darn good reason for her secret?"

"If I uncover the truth, I maybe could fix things for Mom, and she might even let me go to Whitman for soccer this summer. I have a right to know."

ATTA BOY, ROCKY, Dad pipes up, YOU NEED THE TRUTH, BUT OLIVE'S RIGHT. CALLING WON'T WORK. GO TO WHITMAN.

That has been his go-to line for forever. But for once, I don't dismiss his suggestion. After all, the hospital is in Whitman.

Olive says, "Give me time to devise a foolproof plan."

I nod, and we head for our next classes.

In the hallway, I say, *Dad, let's say I agree to go. How am I supposed to get to Whitman?*

I'M NOT SURE. I'M SO SORRY ABOUT EVERYTHING.

I'm a horse's butt for making my dead father apologize to me. I try to lighten the mood with a joke.

Hey, Dad, maybe I should steal the car and drive to Whitman now that I've had so much practice with Uncle Bob. Ha. Ha.

DRIVING IS WICKED DANGEROUS. DO NOT DO THAT. TAKE YOUR BIKE.

Good one, Dad. I chuckle at his wisecrack, but he's not laughing.

CHAPTER 24

I push the hospital letter and Dad's whacky idea to bike to Whitman into a small corner of my brain and pull a tarp over it. It's easy to block stuff like that this week because the dance buzz at school is deafening. People are continuously yakking about their outfits or who they'll dance with.

By Friday, I have to admit I'm pumped too, but my main focus is to cross Max off my problem list.

We eat an early dinner on Friday so I'll have plenty of time to get ready. When I'm dressed, I check myself out in the full-length mirror on the back of the bathroom door. I leave my button-down untucked, but I'm not sure if that look will pass Olive's eagle eye. If I've made a fashion misstep, she's sure to let me know. The black and white-checkered canvas slip-ons Mom thought might not work are totally awesome.

Tonight, I put aside my aversion to hair products and use a dab of gel on my bangs to keep them from flying in every direction while I dance. The stickiness isn't as gross as I remember. I look good and could even pass for a ninth grader.

While I'm admiring myself, Dad weighs in. NICE. YOU AND OLIVE MAKE A CUTE COUPLE. CAN'T WAIT TO SEE THE TWO OF YOU DANCING.

Butt out, puh-leeze.

Having Dad hanging around me at a school dance is the pits. I don't need a chaperone. Most kids were conjuring up arguments to prevent their parents from volunteering at the dance and observing their every move. But I can't prevent my dead father from being there.

OLIVE LIKES YOU, Dad says.

I can't get through to him that his comments about Olive are not wanted. It's bad enough I have to deal with my own thoughts when it comes to her–I don't need his, too.

"Stop! Go away." I speak loudly to emphasize my words.

CAN'T GO AWAY, ROC.

"Okay, I get it, but can you at least stay quiet tonight?"

WILL DO, he promises.

MOM and I pick up Max. As he climbs into the back seat, I introduce them. He didn't get the message about the dress code. He's wearing a light blue polo, khakis and white sneakers. He's out of the loop even though he's been at this school longer than me. He needs an Olive to guide him.

"Where's Olive?" Max asks.

"We're meeting her there." Olive and I had agreed it would be better if no one saw us arriving together.

Mom drops us off and, luckily, she refrains from any gushing because she knows that sort of thing is forbidden when I'm with a friend.

"Let's wait outside for Olive," I tell Max and lean against the brick wall. Max takes a spot next to me. Lots of kids pass by us. After a while, it feels dopey just standing around.

"Never mind, Max. We should go in. She'll text us when she gets here."

"Right." Max follows my lead like I'm the sergeant, and he's a lowly private. That goon who tormented me on my first day at Tucker has disappeared.

Inside the gym, spring is in full fake blossom. The back wall has an enormous mural with skateboarders, flowers and joggers. Bunches of cardboard trees covered with paper green leaves fill the corners. High above us a huge yellow sun floats from the ceiling. There is no lingering odor of sweaty basketball players, rope climbers and wrestlers. I bet the custodian has a special kill-the-gym-smell spray for these non-athletic events.

The place is packed; every middle schooler showed up. Teachers and parents converge in groups around the edges of the room, making sure we don't do anything we're not supposed to. I spot Marco with Tan and some other kids from the Tigers and make a beeline for them. Max trails after me.

"Hey, dude," I say, as a space opens in their circle. I push a couple of guys to make room for Max too. All the boys are in jeans, and two of them are even wearing the exact same blue and green plaid shirts. Nobody speaks to Max. This must be tough for him to be ignored at school. No surprise he wanted to come to the dance with me as his blackmail payment so it would look like he had at least one friend.

Marco spins 360 degrees on one leg and asks, "Where's your date?"

"I don't have a date," I protest, simultaneously giving him a gentle shove.

"But you two are always together," he persists.

"Not always. Where's YOUR girlfriend?"

"Yeah. I wish," Marco says. "Seriously, bro, where's Olive?"

"I haven't seen her. I'll make an announcement on the loudspeaker when she arrives, okay?" I hiss.

"Man, chill." Another kid with bright red hair and a face covered in freckles makes kissing noises in the air like we're in fifth grade, and I'm ready to sock him when the music blasts from the loudspeakers. He and some others move onto the dance floor. It's impossible to hear anyone speaking. I tap Max on the shoulder and nod toward them. He follows me into the middle of a group of seventh graders.

Although I have no idea the name of this dance, I mimic the motions of the kids next to me and jump when they jump. Max copies me. Each time I face in another direction, my eyes scan the room for a skyscraper of a kid, but she's nowhere.

The song goes on forever and when it finishes, Max asks, "What happened to her?"

"Dunno. She abandoned us. I'm going to text her."

No response.

I'm ready to bounce if Max agrees we've been here long enough for me to have fulfilled my part of the bargain.

"Are you ready to go?" I ask him.

"Yup."

"I'll text my mom to pick us up," I say.

Max and I go outside and sit on the grass to wait for her.

"So, are we square after tonight?" I ask.

"Yeah."

"Can I trust that?"

"I'm not that much of a fart-a-fart."

"It's hard being the new kid. You must remember what that's like. Olive told me you came to Milton in fifth grade. Why did you move here anyway?"

"Because my dad changed jobs, but there's more to it. Kind of a secret."

Another family hiding something. This is an epidemic.

"I am an excellent A-1 secret-keeper," I assure him. "To prove it, I'll tell you a secret of mine so we'll have something on the other one." I hope Olive won't mind I'm activating her Nobel prize-worthy secret oath pact without permission.

"Okay, I guess."

I tell Max Dad died, but that the "his heart stopped" story is probably bogus, and there might be something dangerous in Whitman which is why Mom and I had to flee.

"Olive is helping me solve my mystery. Your turn, Max."

He says, "My dad had to change jobs because he was released from jail. He got into trouble in his business. It has to do with taxes, but that's all I know. When he came home, my parents thought we should move."

Double yikes. That's a heck of a secret. "I bet they said it was 'for a fresh start.' That's my mom's favorite line," I say.

"Yeah, something like that. Sorry about your dad. Is he the invisible person you've been talking to?"

"Yup, but it's not how you think. I can explain." Before I utter another word, Mom pulls up, ending our secrets-sharing.

In the car, Max leans over, and his hot breath blows on my neck. "Can I sit with you guys at lunch from now on?" he asks in a small, timid voice.

I could say no because I don't owe him anything anymore, but he needs friends bad. I'm not that heartless. Olive should be okay with it, so I tell him yes. He pats me on the shoulder to seal the deal.

"You guys are leaving early," Mom says, "Didn't you have fun?"

"Oh, yeah, tons of fun." I add a dose of sarcasm because I don't think she deserves to be happy I went to the dance.

"Is Olive staying longer?" she asks.

"She didn't even show up." Those words aren't sharp like before. Now they sound sad.

"That's strange," Mom says.

It sure is. She should've been there, after roping me into going.

When we pull up to Max's house, he says, "Thank you, Rocky's mother."

"You're welcome, Max. You can call me Marybeth."

After he's gone, Mom says, "He seems nice."

"He is." I omit the fact he's a renowned expert in unusual fart names.

When I'm home, I text Olive.

Me: MAD!!!!!!

I add a row of emoji faces with steam shooting out of their nostrils.

The Queen of Fast-repliers falls silent. I text again.

Me: U DIDN'T SHOW!!!!!!!!

I add tons of emojis with exploding heads.

Where is she?

CHAPTER 25

As the first light flows into my room the next morning, I return to consciousness. Through half-opened eyes, I reach for my phone. Still, no messages. Olive fell off the radar completely.

I try to get out of bed, but my legs are tangled in the sheets as if a cyclone whipped through here last night. I thrash around until I free myself and race downstairs to catch Mom before her morning yoga class.

She's drinking coffee in her exercise clothes. I blurt out, "Olive isn't answering my texts."

"Are you concerned?"

"Maybe." I'm working overtime to stay calm and not get hysterical like Mom when she's in full-worry mode, but awful stuff can happen when you least expect it. Mom should know that too.

What if Olive's in some hospital unable to speak, and her parents are demolishing boxes of tissues faster than a wrecking ball? Or maybe it's about her brother.

"Call her house," Mom suggests.

"Why wouldn't she call ME?"

"There could be a simple explanation. Maybe her phone got wet or she lost her charger. Don't jump to conclusions."

She may be right, but I don't want to call Olive's house. I don't respond, and Mom offers to phone for me. I'm grateful I won't be the one that might have to hear bad news which would suck me into a heartbreak tornado.

"Thanks," exhaling air that pricks my mouth with tiny needles as it exits. At this very moment, Mom is Mom. This is how it used to be with us. She always had my back; I trusted her.

She rummages through the junk drawer and finds my class directory. She calls Olive's landline. It rings for a long time. Mom asks if she should leave a voicemail, and I shake my head no. The fact that no one's home early on a Saturday morning isn't a good sign.

Mom and I sit. She rubs my back like I'm five, but I don't mind. My head weighs a ton and floats down to the table. I can't hold it up a minute longer.

In a calm voice, Mom says, "I'm sure she is fi—" She catches herself mid-word and doesn't finish the sentence. She knows as well as I do, you can never be sure things will be fine.

"You're right," I say, lifting my head, but I don't believe that at all.

"I can miss yoga today."

"No. Go. I'm okay. I promise."

Grandpa wanders into the kitchen and pours his coffee. Mom tells him Olive didn't show up at the dance and isn't returning my texts.

"I'm sure she's fine," he says. The word slides out of him as if its path was greased in a thick layer of oil. Doesn't he know "fine" can be a big, ugly lie?

If I was bratty, I'd say "Yeah, right, Grandpa, fine like my dad was supposed to be fine." But Grandpa's doing his best, and it would be some kind of rude to mouth off to him.

Mom leaves for yoga. I go upstairs and text Max to come here. Today, it's me who's in desperate need of a friend. I don't want to be alone and think.

He leaps at my offer and within an hour Max is at the front door. We set up the Xbox to play FIFA soccer. He wins the first game, which surprises me because, number one, I'm an ace at it, and number two, I had no idea he had any soccer skills.

"Do you play real soccer, too?" I ask, as he sets up for our rematch.

"Only fooling around with my dad." His face panic-freezes immediately after he says that. It's a look I'm familiar with. A lot of kids at my old school avoided mentioning their dads to me, because they were afraid I'd dissolve into a puddle, which I wouldn't have. I wanted them to treat me the same, but everything was different after Dad died.

I smile so Max will breathe easy again and say, "You should try out for the Tigers."

"The guys would hate that," he says, "I dug myself into a hole when I moved to Milton. Bad attitude. Forcing you to go to the dance with me was my last hope for a restart."

"Serious though, you'd be a great goalie." I wasn't giving him the business. With his build, he could block anything coming at him. "You can borrow my goalie gloves. They're the bomb. Next season, we'll go to tryouts together."

I can't believe I offered to loan Max, the kid who threatened me, my special gloves. Max's face lights up like it's one gigantic beam coming out of a dark tunnel. He moves toward me as if coming in for a hug, but stops before touching range. A hug is a bit much, so I slap him on the back, which always works with me and Shawny.

Just then, the special text tone I set up for Olive goes off. I drop the game controller and high-five the air, until a sad emoji face appears on my screen. I text her.

Me: ?

Olive: bro sick - explain later

Me: Is he OK?

Olive: Yeah. bad timing

Since the dance, my emotions have cycled between being angry she didn't come, to being sad she didn't come, to being worried she didn't come.

Olive: how was the dance?

Me: great.

I exaggerate.

Olive: missed stepping on your big feet.

She sends an emoji with a devil's face.

Me: HA! can you come over? I have a brand-new plan! Need help!!!!

I was gonna unveil my new idea at the dance, but when she didn't show up, my mind could only focus on what happened to her.

Max and I scarf some cookies while we wait for Olive.

CHAPTER 26

I open the door for Olive, and her eyes latch on to Max who's standing beside me.

"Didn't know you'd be here, Max."

"Yup, I'm here."

The two of them follow me up to my room. Olive drops onto her favorite spot on the floor. Max and I join her there.

"So, dudes, I guess I missed a good time last night."

Max jumps in. "We danced once and left early."

"Hmmm. Rocky, you said it was great without me. Maybe that was a tiny fib." Olive's mouth crooks up into a pretend sneer.

"Why weren't you there?" Max asks.

"I had a family emergency. Before I tell my story, I want to hear Rocky's new plan. You make it sound mysterious. Ooooooo." Olive does a fake-ghost moan, but mostly, it comes off like she's got a bellyache.

"Is this about you-know-who?" Max asks, turning toward me.

"It's okay, Max. Olive's in on everything. She invented the whole secret pact idea." I hope she appreciates I'm giving her props.

"Well, punch me out, Fartfool," Max says, "I knew you weren't smart enough to come up with such a great idea on your own."

Olive might be appalled by his enormous repertoire of fart names and think this is typical boy grossitude. I tell him to knock it off.

"Lighten up, just joking," he says.

Olive ignores him and orders, "Holy shmoly, get to the point already, Rocket Man."

There are three rapid knocks on the door, and Max flinches, grabbing my arm. "Maybe that's him."

"Him who?" I ask.

"Your dad. Maybe he's here now."

"He doesn't knock on doors, and he doesn't make appearances," I explain.

"Calm down, Max Relax." Olive bestows a nickname on him. I hope he appreciates that gift.

"Shush," I whisper-yell to both of them as the door opens.

Mom comes in carrying a huge tray of snacks and drinks which she sets down in the center of the floor. It looks as good as anything Olive's mom prepares.

"Hi, Max. Hi, Olive," Mom says, "Olive, Rocky was worried about you."

Why does she say that to Olive and in front of Max? Worrying about a girl could be a sign we're boyfriend and girlfriend, and we are NOT.

Max flashes a devilish smile. I know he's gonna store this tidbit for future teasing purposes, because I'd do the same thing. You never know when you need something like that in your back pocket.

Olive says, "We had to visit my brother who's away at school. He was in the hospital."

"Is he okay?" Mom asks.

"Turned out to be food poisoning. At first, they were scared it might be his appendix, and he'd need surgery, but no. He was in the hospital overnight."

"I'm glad he's all right," Mom says. "Do you kids want to stay for dinner?"

"I can't," Olive says. "I have all my weekend homework to do."

Max says, "I can't stay either, but thanks for the invitation, Ms. Casson. And thank you for the great food." He's beyond polite. Who is this kid?

Mom leaves, and Max shoves his chunky hand into the popcorn and stuffs his mouth.

"Hey, Max, some of that is for us," Olive warns. "You're so syrupy with Rocky's mom and a big mouth in school. What gives?"

Max swallows, takes a drink and explains, "When you're a new kid, you've got to be tough in school, or people walk all over you. Aren't I right, Rocky?"

"Who gave you that horrible advice? It's screwing with your social life," I say.

"My dad," Max answers.

I'm horrified Max's father would tell him something like that. Maybe his father learned that lesson in prison and passed it along to Max.

"Max, you got a boatload of manure," I say, careful with my language in front of Olive. "Times have changed since your father was in"—here I cough two times so Max understands I'm referring to when his dad was in prison, not when he was in school—"school. No one likes a brute. Right, Olive?"

"Right. Really dumb. Use your head, Maxie," Olive softens her scolding with a sweet name.

"Okay, forget about that. Rocky, what's your new plan?" Max says.

"I'm going to Whitman to talk with a doctor at the hospital that took care of my dad."

"Your mom agreed to take you?" Olive asks.

"No. She doesn't want me anywhere near there. I'm biking."

Olive whips her head toward me. Her eyebrows flare up and then quickly pinch into a unibrow. "That's a colossal monstrosity of an idea."

"It's my only hope. The bike part was my dad's suggestion." I try to make it seem like I have a parent's approval, but I'm not sure if a dead parent counts.

"He really told you, or you're making that up?" Olive asks.

"Absolutely true. At first, I thought he was joking, but he wasn't." I don't add the biking idea came to me at the same time as the not-a-ghost dad said it. He and I are in total sync.

"How far is Whitman?" Max asks.

"About two hours by bike."

"Each way?" Olive's voice is high-pitched, like she saw something frightful.

"Yup," I answer.

Max says, "You can't pedal four hours in one day. I don't believe it."

"Believe it."

"That's a dangerous plan," Olive says. "Do NOT do this."

Does she think I don't know there are risks? I'm super determined, and it outweighs being scared. None of the other plans have worked. I've got to try this. I deserve to know what happened, no matter what.

Olive erupts. "Do not ask me to help you." She's snorting dragon fire, stands up and paces like a caged animal. She might cut and run any second. She won't stop moving. I get up and join her march across my room, pleading with her to stop so I can explain the details.

Finally, she halts and stares me down with large, teary brown eyes. I can't look at her and turn away.

She proclaims. "Not smart, Rocky. I will not be part of this plan. Period."

"But you were pushing me to find out the truth."

"I know. I know, but this is too much, too risky. I'll help you come up with another plan that will be better and safer."

I'm flabbergasted by her intense anger.

"Forget it, then," I say. "So, don't help. I don't give a flying blip." That's a ginormous lie.

"I'm leaving." She heads for the door, saying, "Your obsession is overpowering you and making you do things you shouldn't. I bet your mom will explain what she's keeping from you when you're older."

"I can't wait. The secret is killing me."

"This idea belongs in the trash bin," and she stomps out.

Once she's gone, I refocus on Max.

"Max, I also need you in this plan. You have to cover for me. I'm telling my mom I'm spending Saturday with your family on a day trip to Quincy Market in Boston, and you want me at your house very early that morning."

"We're going there?" he asks. Unlike Olive, this kid needs everything spelled out.

"It's a fake story, Max, but if my mom mentions it to you, you have to play along."

"I'd better not get into any trouble because of this."

"You won't."

I walk him out, and when he's almost at the end of the front walkway, I say, "Sit with us at lunch." He salutes me like I'm his commanding officer, but this time I'm the one who wants his company, because for sure Olive will probably never sit with me again.

Back in my room, all the air leaves my body as if it's a deflating balloon, zipping around the room aimlessly. I collapse to the floor. Under my bed, my soccer bag catches my attention. I drag it out and put on my goalie gloves. They're really clean, practically brand new. When Dad gave them to me, he made sure to point out the thick padding and special grip technology to control the ball. He said every great goalie needs top-of-the-line gloves. Happier times. Not like now.

Dad says, FOUR HOURS ON THE BIKE WILL BE A PIECE OF CAKE, AND AS AN ADDED BONUS, IT'LL HELP YOU GET INTO SHAPE FOR SOCCER.

"I'm a little scared," I say.

BUDDY, FAIL IS NOT IN YOUR DICTIONARY. YOU CAN DO IT.

This bike ride could get me grounded for the rest of my life, and I can kiss goodbye any chance of getting permission for the Whitman soccer clinic. And on top of that I've lost Olive, too.

I hope this bike trip will be worth all that.

ON MONDAY, I enter the cafeteria and spot Olive laughing with a bunch of girls at a table in the middle of the room. A mammoth sweat moustache beads up on my face. I head for "our" table and find Max already there.

He and I "hey" each other. I shovel the food in nonstop as if I just finished a hunger strike. For once, I don't think about the food's color, consistency or contents. I only want to avoid conversation.

Max takes a break from his power-eating and asks, "Is Olive in school today?"

"Yup."

"Where is she?"

"Dunno," I lie.

Max searches the room, and his eyes brighten when they land on Olive as if he found a hidden treasure. "She's sitting with Eva and Gabby. Should I get her?"

"No, you should not. Remember?" My throat closes, and I put down the fork, unable to take another bite.

"You mean about—" Max says.

"Quiet." I interrupt him before he says something he shouldn't and add a swift kick under the table.

"So, she's staying mad at you?"

"Yup."

The rest of our lunch passes in silence.

ALL WEEK I work on my prep list for Saturday's bike ride to Whitman. Olive would have made sure I didn't forget anything, but I do the best I can to be responsible and write down all the details.

This is my list so far:

1. Check bike tire pressure
2. Put hospital address in GPS
3. Make sure Shawn's address is in my phone
4. Pack snacks and water bottle
5. Think of questions to ask the doctor

Friday night, I get into bed and ask Dad, "Any second thoughts about this trip?"

No response.

I try once more to contact him. "Are you absolutely, positively sure this is worth it? If you say don't go, I'll abort the launch."

Still no answer. The mission is on.

I wish it was Sunday already, and the bike trip was over. I'd be safely home with the truth.

CHAPTER 21

I blast out of bed at 6:00 on Saturday. I feel like I've been waiting for this day for forever. I re-check the forecast in case I need to adjust the number of layers I wear. No rain today, cool but not cold. All systems are go.

My plan to grab a tube of yogurt and a jam-filled cereal bar and leave is thwarted when Mom's in the kitchen to fix me a "good" breakfast. I gobble the food to get out of there before she detects my deception.

When she hugs me goodbye, it takes a ton of willpower not to cave and confess everything. I guess I'm not as professional at secret-keeping as she is. Then to make me feel even more like a weasel, she gives me spending money for my fake trip into Boston with Max's family. My mom-lies are burying me under a heaping pile of steamy guilt.

I walk my bike out of the garage, check my cell's GPS to make sure it's set for Kenmore Hospital, and I'm off. Barely two blocks from my house, my phone pings with Olive's text tone. This is the first time she's contacted me all week. I pull over to the curb to read her message.

Olive: Call me

Me: Can't. on my way.

Olive: CALL ME! PLEASE!

I take note of the all caps and exclamation points.

Me: why?

Olive: IMPORTANT!!!!!!!

I phone her.

"Wassup?" I say.

Her noisy breathing sounds thick, like it's covered in the gross mucus you get from a cold. She's speechless, a rare condition for her.

"Out with it." This delay is getting annoying.

"Don't go," she squeaks with little mouse-like noises.

"This bike trip is my last, best hope to get some answers."

There's another long pause as if each word she wants to say is so precious she can't bear to part with it. Finally, in slow motion, she says, "DO NOT go through with this plan, or I WILL tell your mother!"

Wha-at! I rip off my helmet and hurl it to the ground, screaming into the phone, "Why are you threatening me? Okay, you don't want to help or be my friend, but you are committing sabotage."

I can't believe Olive would be so disloyal. Squealing is a serious offense. There's no coming back from that.

"Why would you do that?" My voice tears out of my throat and dumps its anger on her.

In contrast, her tone is barely audible. "Rocky, this trip is way too risky. Cars whiz by, and sometimes they don't notice the bikers."

I can't believe I have to explain this to her. "You, of all people, should understand why I have to do this. We tried other ideas, and all of them failed."

"We'll figure out a better plan. I promise," she says.

"No. You don't have to be on board, but do NOT tell my mother. Even my dad's encouraging me to do this. It's THAT important."

"You can't rely on a voice in your head. That's ridiculous."

"I'm not relying on it. I'm just saying he and I are on the same page. And remember, we have a pact to keep each other's secrets."

"Don't you care about your mom? If you get hurt or lost, she'll be devastated. I have some experience with stuff like this. My parents went berserk until they found my brother after he took off. Even though they were big-time mad, they were so relieved when they found out he was okay. Parents are like that. This crazy trip could get you sent to a special school, too."

She might be right. This might be the worst thing I ever do, but I have to crack open Mom's secrets no matter the price.

"Nothing's gonna happen to me," I say, "I'll be back before my mom finds out. I'm not doing this to go to a concert like your brother did. My dad died under mysterious circumstances. I have to know what I'm up against here."

Olive says, "But because I know your plan, I'm sort of involved even if I don't want to be. So, it'd be my fault too if something bad happens. Please don't go."

I wish I could tell her I won't, but I'm the son. If anyone deserves the truth, it's me. She forces me into hyper-cruel mode. I say, "If you rat me out, I'll blab all over school about your brother."

"I don't care. This, you, are too important. Go ahead and tell."

Wow, that was not the response I expected. I need an even more powerful threat to keep her from snitching to Mom. "I'll spill Max's secret too." As I utter those words, the rat inside me emerges to gnaw at Olive. I know she'd hate to be responsible for ruining Max's life at Tucker.

"No. No. Don't do that. Whatever Max's secret is, I don't want it broadcast on account of me. I couldn't live with myself. Max can be a real jerk, but he has potential."

"I'll be fine," I say, turning on the kinder and gentler version of me. "There's hardly any traffic on a Saturday," I reassure her, "And I'll stay off the main highway. I'll be super careful."

"But it's so far."

"I guarantee I'll be one hundred percent safe. Do you want me to text you every half hour to prove I'm okay?"

"Will you? Don't forget. If you don't, I might panic."

"I won't forget. Text you soon. Bye."

"Bye. Rocky, I lov...I love getting your texts."

I retrieve my helmet and check my phone. That delay lasted fifteen minutes, so my schedule should be okay, but I'd better not linger on my rest stops.

I fling my leg over the bike's bar with renewed energy now that Olive and I are in a better place. My heart settles into a normal rhythm, and my pedaling keeps pace with it.

Dad says, BE HAPPY SHE CARES ABOUT YOU.

"Yeah. But can we not talk about her?" No matter how often I tell him Olive is off limits, he doesn't let up. The trouble is, I can't ignore him, and I can't stop him from talking. I'm totally stuck with Dad living in my head.

It's early, and the morning fog covers the houses in an out-of-focus haze. The road's still damp from overnight sweat. I keep my headlight on for added safety. I DO plan to come home in one piece today. A few cars pass me, but the traffic is light.

The GPS lady alerts me to turn right in a few miles and get on Route 28, the old road from Milton to Whitman, which isn't much used anymore since most people prefer the speed of a major highway. It will be longer, but much safer. See Olive, you didn't need to worry. I'm cautious.

After a while, I check my phone. A half hour has passed since Olive and I spoke. I stop for a drink, remove my hoodie and tie it around my waist. I paste on a huge smile, take a selfie and text it to Olive with a thumbs-up emoji and the hashtag #safebiketrip.

She texts back a happy face and an I'M SORRY in all caps.

No prob. I text back.

Back on the road, the GPS is silent because it's a straight ride for the next fourteen miles until Exit 16. So far, the road has been pretty flat, and the biking is like gliding on slick ice. No obstacles and no bumps.

At my next rest stop, I send Olive another selfie. This time, I make a goofy face.

Again, she texts back a happy face emoji.

I gobble an energy bar, as Dad says, YOU'RE ALMOST THERE, ROCKY.

"Yup."

ARE YOU NERVOUS ABOUT WHAT YOU MIGHT FIND OUT? he asks.

"Should I be?"

SECRETS CAN BE GREAT LIKE A CHRISTMAS PRESENT STASHED IN THE CLOSET, OR THEY CAN BE BAD LIKE YOU FIND OUT YOUR LONG-LOST RELATIVE IS A SERIAL MURDERER. NO MATTER WHAT, REMEMBER YOU'RE MY NUMBER ONE SON.

"Jeez, Dad, I know that."

When the GPS lady announces a left turn at the next light, I take my last rest stop. After this, it isn't much farther to the hospital. Instead of texting, I call Olive.

"Is-everything-all right?" Olive's words come out at breakneck speed.

"Why do you sound so strange?" I ask.

"I got scared because you called instead of texting."

"I'm fine. I'm almost there. Any last-minute advice?"

"No. Good luck. I mean that."

"Thanks. Bye."

I put the phone in my backpack, drink some water and prepare to ride the final few miles to Whitman.

CHAPTER 28

S oon, some of the streets begin to look familiar. I pedal past my old library where I spent many hours scooched between Dad's legs with my head against his chest listening to the librarian read *Caps for Sale* and *Harold and the Purple Crayon*. Two of my all-time favs. I knew them by heart.

I turn right onto a wide street with huge trees on either side whose overhanging branches form a green roof blocking the sky. The houses are set far back from the road with enormous front lawns. If I had to cut the grass for one of those monsters, I'd demand a rider mower.

I don't remember any hospitals near my old neighborhood. A couple of years ago, I broke my arm, and the emergency room they took me to was nowhere near here.

There aren't any large buildings in sight and no street signs with a giant H, which indicate a hospital nearby. Is it even possible for the GPS to be wrong? Doubtful, but it could be my input error. I stop and lean by the curb to fish around in my backpack for my phone.

I press the home button, but the screen stays black. I hold the power button down to reboot which is often the best fix, but nothing happens. Then I press both buttons at the same time. It's completely dead. I must've left something on after my last stop that sucked up all the battery juice. How could I be so friggin' careless? I got sloppy. Holy crap!

Without my GPS, I might not find the hospital, and for sure I won't find my way back to Milton. Mr. Handler might have been right after all. I'm in need of an old-fashioned map.

My only option will be to sneak over to Shawn's after the hospital and get him to print out directions. It will be a masterful stroke of luck to accomplish that without his mother seeing me. Now, I have to keep my focus on finding the hospital or this entire quest will join my other efforts in the dumpster.

I say, "This plan was going too perfectly until now. Right, Dad?"

I guess the not-a-ghost dad doesn't have any advice how to get out of this mess, so he stays quiet.

I'm about to give up on my attempt to find the hospital and accept this as another failure, when at last a sign appears. It's very low to the ground and in a brownish-gray color that blends in with the surrounding tree bark. A camouflage artist must have designed it. There's no mention of a hospital, just the words Kenmore Facility, but that can't be a coincidence.

The driveway curves to the left. After I pass a high fence of tall evergreens, a red brick mansion, where a rock star or a billionaire might live, comes into view. There aren't any ambulances parked in front, and no people go in or out. It's kind of desolate. The windows are tinted dark, so you can't see inside. There's definitely an element of spook here.

I lean my bike against the building and walk up a few stairs to the door. The knob doesn't turn. I didn't think hospitals are ever locked. There's a buzzer to my right with a small sign: Ring for Entrance. For some reason, people aren't allowed to walk right in.

I press the buzzer, aware that I'm here completely cut off without a phone. If anything happens to me, I can't be tracked. Olive is right, Mom would be destroyed, even if she's responsible for me being in this predicament. All my sneaking around is her fault.

A skinny woman with tiny dark eyes and a long, narrow nose opens the door part-way. She checks me out, gazing around as if someone might be behind me; I'm guessing she expects to see a grown-up with me.

She isn't wearing a uniform. When I broke my arm, all the doctors and nurses who took care of me in the hospital wore white coats or uniforms.

"Can I help you?" she asks. She keeps the door partially open and doesn't invite me inside. I can't believe Dad had to stay in a creepy place like this.

"My name is Rock...I mean Ronald Casson, Junior, and I'd like to speak with Doctor Sandler."

"Do you have an appointment?"

"No."

"Are you here to visit someone who's staying with us?" Her eyes never blink once and burn straight through me. She isn't happy with this intrusion. I try not to let her intimidate me.

"No."

"Sorry, Dr. Sandler isn't available today, and he never sees anyone without an appointment. I can take a message for him."

After this whole difficult journey, I'm gonna come up empty-handed. I went through a lot to get here. At a time like this, I desperately need Olive's sharp mind. I remember how quickly she came up with the fake science report idea so I could go camping with Uncle Bob.

Boom! Fake report. What a brainstorm. If that scheme worked once, why not try it again? I tell the lady I'm doing a report for school, and I need information about what kind of place Kenmore Facility is. I give myself a virtual pat on the back for coming up with this genius save.

The lady's lips move from a long straight line into a slight upturn, which makes her a lot less scary. Still, she doesn't ask me in, but she comes out to join me on the top step, closing the door behind her.

"Why didn't you say that? You don't need the doctor for that. I can help you. We treat people with problems—"

I interrupt her, "Like heart problems?"

"No, this is a hospital for mental health issues."

"What?" That doesn't sound right. Why would Dad be in a mental health hospital? There's some mistake, or I'm misunderstanding her, so I ask, "What other kinds of sicknesses do you take care of?"

"Nothing else. We do have a therapeutic school on the property for young people, but this building is the hospital."

I don't need a mirror to know my mouth is hanging open.

The woman continues, "Kenmore Hospital treats people with mental health problems. We've been here for years, and we are a good neighbor. You should write that in your report."

My breathing stops. I have to concentrate to drag air into my lungs so I can speak again. "I will include that for sure. Is it possible some people with heart problems would come here for treatment?"

"They'd go to Central Hospital on the other side of town."

The name clicks as soon as she says it. It's where I got the cast put on my arm. I remember they offered me candy from a basket with the words "Central Hospital" printed on the wrappers.

I ask, "Can you describe some of the illnesses you treat here? I want to put that in my report."

"Why don't you mention a few of the more well-known diagnoses, such as depression, anxiety and obsessive-compulsive disorder."

I nod.

"Don't you want to write this all down? You can come in to get a paper and pen," she offers.

I regain my composure before she hauls me inside. "That's not necessary," I stammer, "I have an excellent memory. Thank you for your help."

"You're welcome. Good luck with your assignment."

She swipes a card to re-open the door and disappears inside. I stumble down the stairs, lift up my bike and ram it into the building with all my strength. Back and forth. Back and forth, until my arms are ready to fall off. I drop it and crumple on the ground, hugging my knees tightly and rocking on my bottom to soothe myself.

Kenmore is a mental hospital, which means Dad had mental problems in addition to a bad heart. It was the biggest of big secrets.

Dad speaks in a soft voice. ROCKY, BE GLAD YOU'RE FINALLY CLOSER TO SOLVING THE MYSTERY.

With all my guessing what might have happened, I never thought of this. Dad acted quirky at times. He could be hyper or lie on the couch for days like he was paralyzed. He might be unpredictable and often had whacky ideas of stuff we should do. Mom thought his projects were too much. If all that was because he was sick, he should've told me.

I drag myself to my feet and climb on the bike, but the front wheel doesn't move. The dented fender digs into the tire, and the rim is bent. I abandon the bike and walk up the driveway. I came here for the truth, but not this truth.

I want to go home.

CHAPTER 29

Putting one leg before the other requires supreme effort. My head throbs as if I had rammed it into the wall instead of my bike. Thoughts crash in my brain at breakneck speed. They're going so fast, it's impossible to capture one thought for more than a second, before a new one barges in to take its place.

I turn down Babcock Road and then onto Abbottsford. The For Sale sign is still poking out of the front lawn, but now there's a Sold sign swinging from the bottom of it. That red, four-letter word kills my dream of moving back to Whitman. This house belongs to another family.

The place looks abandoned. I guess the new people have the good sense not to move until the school year's finished. I grab the bottom of my t-shirt and dab at the moisture running over my bottom eyelids and dripping down my cheeks.

I walk around to the back and pass the spot where Dad carved our initials into the wet cement against Mom's specific orders. But when she saw the heart surrounding the letters of our names, her anger melted away. "Oh, Ron, it's sweet," she said.

Dad replied, "MB, the three of us will be here forever," and then he hugged her, lifting her off the ground. He put her down and reached for me, swinging me around faster and faster until the two of us were super dizzy and fell on the grass.

Now I sit on the deck steps, Dad's deck, as we called it, because he started the project. Sadness seeps into my body, filling all available empty spaces. I cry until my eyes run dry and burn hot like the waves of orangish sands in the Sahara Desert.

I jiggle the backdoor handle, though I doubt it would be unlocked. It doesn't open, but that's no problem for me. The new owners would have no clue that a locked door can't keep me out of my own house. Thanks to another of Dad's when-Mom-is-away experiments, I know how to break-in.

Dad wanted to test our house to make sure it was burglar-proof. First, he slammed his shoulder into the front door until he howled in pain and then announced it passed the test. The backdoor also held firm. Next, Dad moved on to the basement's little windows. He sat on the ground, put his feet up against the glass and pushed. The window popped open.

"Aha," he said. "This isn't good."

"But no adult could fit through that window," I told him. "The burglar would get stuck half-way in and half-way out. It'd be easy for the police to catch him."

Then, with a wicked grin, Dad said, "But what if the robber brought his young son with him? I'll lower you in. Sit on the ground and stick your feet through the opening. I'll hold you and ease you down."

Dad gripped me under both shoulders and guided me in feet first.

Once I was inside, Dad pushed his face through the opening and said, "By the way, a real burglar wouldn't bring his kid. Just joking. The house is deemed break-in proof. Mission accomplished."

I sit in front of the same basement window and push on it. It doesn't budge. I move in closer and bend my knees for more leverage. This time using a little too much strength, the glass shatters in a loud crash. I kick out the couple of spiky pieces remaining and slide in.

First thing I do is rub my hands over the rainbow wall that Dad and I painted, as if I can absorb the colors through my skin. I make sure to touch each color and make my wish. If you forget any one of them, your wish is ruined. Today, I don't even know what to wish for.

I head upstairs and lean under the kitchen faucet to drink. All the water that poured out of my eyes might've dehydrated me. I splash my face and shake off the excess water like a dog coming out of the ocean.

I peek into each room on the first floor before going upstairs. In my old room I see the outlines on the walls where my Man U and Real Madrid posters used to hang. I bet if I got a body x-ray there would also be an outline in me where my heart used to be. Now, I can't feel my heart at all.

Of all the places in the world where I should be warm and happy, it would be in this room. But its emptiness gives me the chills. It's a stinging reminder of all I have lost.

I crouch down to inspect the baseboard in the corner where I wrote my secret lists of friends in the order I liked them. I did that every year since third grade, and Shawn's name was always number one, but if I make a new list now, I might put Olive first.

Then, I perch on the window sill and check out the big, old oak climbing tree. It might've grown since we left. I visualize Dad and me sitting on its branches, but my memories are disturbed when a loud noise comes from across the street.

My old neighbor, Mr. Novick, shuffles this way as fast as he can, banging his cane hard with each step. The noise of the breaking glass must have been louder than I thought.

I dash into my closet and curl into a tight ball, making myself as small and unnoticeable as possible. I wish I had a genie or fairy godmother to make me invisible.

No doubt I'll get caught. Even the tiniest bit of luck I might have had is being drowned under the dark storm cloud hovering above and drenching me in torrential tears.

There's no one to rescue me.

CHAPTER 30

The sound of Mr. Novick's heavy, uneven footsteps moving from room-to-room on the first floor reach me in the closet.

Dad! I shout silently for my not-a-ghost father. *Help me!*

He says, STAY QUIET AND HOPE MR. NOVICK'S BUM LEG WON'T LET HIM MAKE IT UP THE STAIRS.

I pray Dad's right, but it's kind of evil to want Mr. Novick's wounded leg to be giving him that much pain. Mr. Novick once lifted his pants and showed me a map of twisty scars from the leg operations he had in the army.

Mr. Novick yells, "You kids are not supposed to be in here. Come out this minute!" He tries to sound menacing, which he isn't at all. His long white beard and big belly remind me of Santa Claus without the red suit. He always brought me his leftover Halloween candy, and he never complained that my friends and me were too loud when we played outside.

I shut my eyes like a little kid playing hide-and-seek, hoping if I don't see him, he won't see me. I wait, but in no time, his feet thud up the stairs. I'm not really surprised. Nothing is going my way today.

My bedroom door opens with a bang. Mom used to yell at me for smashing the door into the wall, because once the knob left a deep dent that is still visible if you know where to look. After that, I was more careful.

Mr. Novick's cane pounds the floor as he shouts, "Who's in here? Come out immediately, or I'm calling the police."

The police? Oh, no!

His cane pushes open the closet's folding door. He thrusts his stick around until it smacks me squarely on the top of my head.

"Got you! Get out of there! Hello, Police."

If I'm arrested, Mom will kill me for sure, so I rush out and show myself, saying, "Don't call the cops, Mr. Novick. It's only me, Rocky."

He doesn't even have a phone in his hand. It's a giant bluff.

"Rocky?" His eyes blink fast, then slow and fast again like he's sending signals to someone. He repeats my name as if he can't believe he heard correctly. Maybe he doesn't recognize me. He seems confused.

I stand up a little straighter and say, "Yup, it's Rocky." It hasn't been that long, so he should recognize it's the real me.

He says, "I'm surprised to find you here. Some kids have been eyeing this place since it has been empty and planning mischief. I shout at them to stay away, but I thought they found some opening and got in. I forgot my phone and had to pretend to call the police. What are you doing here?"

"I wanted to visit my old house again, so I snuck in. Sorry."

"Are you all right? I heard glass breaking."

"I'm okay. No bruises or cuts." I lift my arms and twirl them in front of him to prove it.

"Are you here by yourself?"

"Uh huh."

"Does your Mom know where you are?"

"No."

"How did you get here?" he asks.

"Bike."

"I didn't see any bike when I circled the house."

"It broke down, and I had to walk the rest of the way." I shudder remembering the banged-up wreckage I left on the grass near the hospital. Like me, my bike took quite a beating today. Thinking about that mangled hunk of metal makes my eyes and nose drip in unison. I raise the end of my shirt to wipe them when Mr. Novick pulls out a handkerchief and hands it to me. I swab wherever I'm leaking.

Mr. Novick says, "Oh, Rocky, this must be very difficult for you. Losing a parent is bad enough without having to deal with suicide too. It's a troubling thing to comprehend, especially for a kid."

What the heck, Mr. Novick! He's gone senile since we moved. He's not making sense.

I try to be gentle, because clearly his mind is fizzled. "Mr. Novick, don't you remember my dad died from a heart problem?"

His cheeks turn as white as his beard. He stammers, "But. But."

I try hard to speak in a normal tone so I don't frighten him. "Maybe you're confusing my dad with someone else."

His beard quivers, his mouth opens, but no sound comes out. He leans against the wall for support. I'm afraid he might fall. He says, "I thought you knew. Rocky, I'm so sorry. I thought you knew. I wish I could swallow back my words."

My legs cramp with a shooting pain that reaches my toes. What Mr. Novick said is impossible. Wouldn't I have picked up some clues that Dad had problems like that? People don't just decide one day to do that. I knew Mom was hiding the truth, but in a million, billion, gazillion years or whatever the biggest amount is, actually no number in the world, would I suspect that was her secret.

Words can't be re-swallowed, and secrets can't be re-secreted. Once they're exposed, you can't go back to unknowing. I almost laugh out loud thinking how hard I worked to learn the truth, and now I don't even want it.

The white parts of Mr. Novick's eyes grow larger. He appears quite terrified, as if he's the one in trouble for breaking the window.

"Please forgive me. You should call your mother," he begs.

My legs finally unlock, and I slump to the floor. My head sinks onto my knees, and then the dam bursts. The faucets open, and water pours out of my eyes.

Mr. Novick lowers himself to the floor, groaning, and puts his arm around me, which only makes me cry harder.

"Please call your mother," he pleads. "She needs to be with you now."

"Mr. Novick." *Sob*. "Did. You. Know. My. Dad." *Sob*. "Was. In. Kenmore Hospital?" As I talk, I don't even recognize my own voice.

"I'm not saying anything more. You have to talk to your mother."

Dad loved me and Mom. He said it again and again. I believed him; I still believe him. He couldn't have done what Mr. Novick said he did, could he? And what if he did? What if he was sad because of the time I told him he couldn't come to my games anymore without my permission. I was mad because he missed a championship soccer game for a phony excuse, or so I thought. Once, I teased him for days about how he couldn't finish any projects. Did I make him so sad?

My mean words must've pricked Dad as they exited my mouth as if they had stingers attached like those killer hornets who attacked Uncle Bob. How could I have been so ignorant? But they should've told me. I'm the son. I should've known.

Mr. Novick keeps asking me to go with him to his house so we can call Mom. I stand, and he struggles to get to his feet, but his wonky leg and fat stomach are too much to overcome, and he plops down.

After a couple of misguided attempts, I stretch out my hand for him to grab. He gets halfway up when gravity pulls him down and me on top of him. I land on his belly, trampoline off and roll onto the floor onto my bottom and start laughing, but it's not a normal, healthy laugh. The sound is wild and loud like my crying was a few minutes earlier.

Mr. Novick huffs, "Go to my house and bring a dining room chair with arms. I can use it to pull myself up."

"Okay."

As I head downstairs, the not-a-ghost dad murmurs something, but I can't understand him because his words are mingled with sobs too.

Finally, he says, MOM WILL HELP YOU. YOU CAN COUNT ON HER.

I know.

I'm tempted to ask him if he loved me, but for sure, I know what his answer would be.

At the bottom of the stairs, I'm startled by a frantic, heavy pounding on the front door. Someone else is trying to break-in.

CHAPTER 31

Frightened, I race back to Mr. Novick, but stop first on the landing to peek out of the little round window. In sixth grade, this was my afternoon lookout post for a month when that pest Emily Pastern came by uninvited. I'd pretend not to be home. Eventually, she gave up on me and fixated on another "lucky" boy.

I crouch down and inch my eyes upward until I glimpse a woman banging fiercely on the door and yelling to open it. Then she calls out my name. Who would know I'm here? She tilts her head for a brief second, and I recognize Shawn's mother. I dash down to open the door for her.

"Rocky, are you okay?" She grabs me by both shoulders and sticks her face right into mine, as if she's hunting for something she lost in my eyeballs. I don't know what that could be.

"Yes, I'm fine, but Mr. Novick's on the floor upstairs." She follows me to my old bedroom.

"What are you doing down there, Edward?" she asks.

Mr. Novick replies, "I sat down to keep Rocky company, and I'm stuck here."

"Rocky, we'll help him up together," Ms. R. instructs. "And Edward, you try to stand when we pull you."

"Right," he agrees. "I'm sorry for all the trouble I've caused."

We get on each side of him and place an arm under his armpit. When Ms. R. gives the signal, we hoist him up. I pass Mr. Novick his cane so he can steady himself. I put my hand under his elbow to give him extra support.

Ms. R. takes out her phone and her thumbs fly over the letters as she texts. I don't need three guesses to know who's on the other end of those messages.

When she finishes, she says in the firm voice of a person in charge, "Rocky, we'll walk Mr. Novick home and then go to my house to wait for your mother."

Mr. Novick turns the doorknob on his house and fixes his lost, sad puppy eyes on me. He says, "I'm so, so sorry."

"It's okay," I say.

Then once again, he asks to be forgiven. I say sure. I'm not mad at him.

Once it's only the two of us, Ms. R. asks me, "Why does Edward, I mean Mr. Novick, keep apologizing to you?"

"It's nothing." I don't plan on asking her anything, even though I suspect she knows a lot more than I do. I have a ton of questions floating in my head. Who am I if I have a Dad who killed himself? Am I still his number one son? Do I want to be his number one son?

The not-a-ghost dad isn't speaking to me. Perhaps he's too scared to "face me."

My questions form at a furious pace, as if I'm a detective grilling a criminal in a police station. What is the matter with me? Why was I in such a thick fog when it came to Dad? Was I too occupied with myself? Did Mom make our life too normal? Max was right, I'm the biggest fartwad to ever walk the face of the earth.

When Ms. R. opens her door, I ask, "Is Shawn home?" I hope so hard her answer is no.

"He's at the movies. He'll be home in a couple of hours."

She probably thinks I'm disappointed, but Shawny isn't the type of guy you need at a time like this. Max might understand better, because he's been through some pretty tough stuff in his own life. Right now, though, it's better I'm alone. My brain is fried.

Once we're inside Ms. R.'s kitchen, she makes a phone call.

"He's here," she says in the quiet, calm voice moms use to soothe an upset kid.

Pause.

"Okay."

Pause.

"No, he didn't say."

Long pause.

"Edward keeps apologizing."

Pause.

"Don't know."

Pause.

"Quiet. Very quiet."

Pause.

"Drive carefully, MB. See you soon."

She puts down the phone and says, "You must be starved."

"Just thirsty." The crying and runny nose have left me dry.

"Lemonade or OJ?"

"Water, please."

She hands me a glass, and I down the whole thing without taking a break. I hope refilling my tank doesn't restart the bawling. There's been too much crying already today.

"Do you want to watch TV or play with Shawn's Xbox until your mom comes?"

"Can I wait in there?" I point to the den where Shawn and I hang when we're not in his room.

"Sure. Call me if you need anything. I'll be right here."

I drop onto the sofa, and my head flops onto its rounded, soft arm. The urge to sleep overcomes me, but I'm not ready to give in to it. I ask in a hushed voice, "Dad, are you here?"

No answer.

"Dad, I wish you hadn't done that. I miss you so bad."

No response from him.

My eyes close, and I picture Dad with outstretched arms as if he wants to hug me, but he doesn't come close. Maybe he's afraid of my reaction.

The next thing I'm aware of is a hand gently rubbing my shoulder, accompanied by a voice saying, "Sweetheart. I'm here."

My eyes fight against the urge to open them. Gravity's determined they stay shut, but with lots of effort I raise the lids and try to focus. Mom is standing in front of me. I fling myself into her arms. She squeezes me to her, and I cry again. The harder I sob, the tighter she holds me. I don't pull away.

"Honey, it'll be okay," she promises.

"Will it?" I ask when I'm able to speak again.

"Yes."

"How did you find out I was in Whitman?" I ask, still wrapped in her arms.

"Olive called me. She told me you biked to Kenmore Hospital and had stopped answering your phone. She was frantic when you didn't text or call her."

"The battery died. Sorry."

"I knew it would take me almost an hour to drive here, so I asked Rochelle to look for you at the hospital."

"Did she see my bike?" I ask, knowing the sight of that twisted mess would be pretty alarming to anyone.

"She found your bike all bent, but no sign of you. I guessed you went to our old house. Rochelle went there to check. What made you take such a chance and ride your bike so far?"

I suck in some snot and say, "I had to talk to someone at the hospital. I didn't believe the story that Dad's heart just stopped, and I didn't understand why we had to move so fast and why I couldn't go to the soccer clinic this summer. There was something awful you weren't telling me. When I accidentally found a letter that Dad had been in Kenmore Hospital, I knew for sure there was a terrible secret."

"Oh, Rocky, I'm so sorry. I didn't want you to find out like this."

I continue to lay out everything for her. "It was the final proof of a humongous secret. Mr. Novick found me in the house and accidentally told me how Dad died. He was certain I already knew."

My eyes drop to the floor. "I should've known."

Mom looks sick and in pain at the same time like a person who had a major operation. "I made a huge mistake," she says, "Dad and I had discussed when we would explain his mental illness to you and how it affected him when he wasn't doing well. He wanted us to wait until you were at least in high school. We're guilty of a giant cover-up. We didn't appreciate how much you had grown in every way. You'll have to forgive me."

"Does everyone know about the you-know-what except me? Even Shawn?" It would be major unfair if I was the only person who didn't know.

"Shawn doesn't know. That's why we moved. I was scared someone would let it slip and it would get around town. There are people who attach a stigma to mental illness. Do you understand what that means?"

"I'm no dunce, Mom, I know that word."

Sniffling, I reach for my shirt and dry my face like I've been doing so many times today. The fabric is soggy and yucky.

"Why didn't you tell me about IT right after it happened?"

Mom puts my chin in her hand and tilts my face up so we look eyeball-to-eyeball. "You can say the word. Dad died of suicide. Sometimes people with mental health problems get hopeless, and they make that choice in the moment. But many people never ever consider suicide, even if they have the same illness Dad had. I never thought Dad would get to that point, but he did."

"Sui...cide." The word comes out of my mouth sliced into two parts as if it will fit better in smaller pieces.

Mom releases me from her embrace. "Dad and I agreed long ago to shield you. I guess I thought I should keep our bargain even after he died. I should've made another choice. I couldn't think straight for a while. It was such a shock."

"You mean he never said anything to you about doing what he did?"

"The possibility was in the back of my mind, but no, I didn't see it coming." She clenches and unclenches her fists as her knuckles whiten. There's something more she isn't telling me even now.

"So maybe I'm the absolute cruelest son in this world or on any planet with life on it, because I got mad at him for missing my big game."

As an avalanche of guilt smothers me, I continue, "And then there was the time"

"Dad was ill. Nothing you did caused this illness. I should have told you. Rocky, forgive me. Please forgive me." Her eyes glisten, and she squeezes her face muscles to hold back the tears. I recognize the method.

"When Dad was in the hospital," she says, "we'd tell you he was on a business trip. It was complicated. We were protecting you and him too, in a way. Sometimes people don't understand mental illness. They don't realize it's like cancer, diabetes or even a stroke. Someone gets sick, and they can't pinpoint where it came from. They get treatment, which doesn't always work.

"When it's suicide, some people want to blame the person who died or someone else for it, or they try to compile a person's whole life into that one act."

"And you thought I wouldn't understand?"

"We wanted to wait until you were older to explain. I misjudged the situation, and mostly, I misjudged you."

"Can we go to Grandpa's now? My head hurts," I say. "I need some thinking time."

Mom takes my hand and leads me into the kitchen. "Thank you, Rochelle. We're leaving. I'll be in touch."

She hugs Shawn's mom, who turns to me and says, "Sorry you missed Shawn, but rain check. Come stay for a weekend."

Mom answers, "Yes, that would be great for both of them. We'll put it on the calendar soon. Thanks."

So, I guess my being in Whitman is safe again now. I had hoped to be able to come back here ever since we moved, but it isn't important anymore.

In the car, Mom says, "Biking to Whitman was dangerous."

"It wasn't only my idea. Someone important helped me come up with that plan."

"Who? Max?"

I smile for the first time since I sent that silly selfie to Olive earlier. "I wouldn't exactly call Max an important person."

"I don't believe Olive would suggest that."

"No, she hated the idea. It was Dad." I pause to let it sink in.

Mom glances over at me, then puts her eyes back on the road. She echoes what I just said but adds a question mark at the end. "It was Dad?" She sounds like she doesn't believe her ears.

"Sort of. Can we talk about that later?"

"Rocky, are you sure you're okay?"

"I had to learn the truth, and now I did. Not ready to talk more now."

"Of course. No rush. I'm here."

Mom goes silent, and the voice of my dead father fills the empty space. I think he's weepy. He says, I'M SORRY, ROCKY. I WISH I HAD—

A sonic boom in my head drowns out whatever he was going to

say. It's like a bomb explodes and scatters me into a million pieces. I squeeze my eyes and breathe in deeply through my mouth trying to suck back all the little bits of me floating in the debris to remake one whole Rocky.

CHAPTER 32

Grandpa's waiting for us in the doorway. This time, he doesn't pat my head. He hugs me, which brings on more out-of-control crying. We stand together for a long time until my tears trickle to a stop.

He speaks first. "You're a strong kid, Rocky. I guess your dad knew that when he gave you the nickname of a real champion who is tough and undefeated. It fits you perfectly." He lowers his face and kisses the top of my head. More than once.

"Grandpa, need to go to my room. Don't worry, I'm fine."

"Sure," he says.

Mom follows me upstairs. I dive under the covers and pull them around me tight in a mummy-wrapping. She sits beside me and pushes the hair off my forehead with a warm hand. Her eyes and mouth sag as if sadness is melting her face.

Mom says, "I'm surprised someone at the hospital would talk to you about Dad without me present. That place can be a little scary at first."

"Boy, it sure is. When I discovered the building was locked, it seemed even more eerie, but I was determined to find out the truth. I had to summon a mountain of courage to ring that buzzer. A woman came out to talk to me.

"I didn't mention Dad was in her hospital. I made up a story that I needed information for a school report. That's how I found out what types of illnesses they treat there. Do they keep the door locked because it's a mental hospital?"

"Yes. They don't want people roaming around or coming in when they aren't supposed to."

"Oh. And please don't be angry with Mr. Novick. He was shocked that I was shocked. He's upset he let it slip out."

Mom's face pretzel-twists, making her eyes, nose and mouth scrunch together and meet in the middle. "I'm not mad at him. I'm mad at me. I should've told you right after Dad died. All those years of deception were ingrained in me. I was on auto-pilot and couldn't see how to take control and change direction.

"Mental illness can be more difficult to understand than some physical illnesses. And it's sad when people believe the person who has the disease could get better if they only tried harder. Dad seemed to be improving with new pills his doctor had prescribed."

I'm trying real hard to understand and make sense of all this new info. "Why did you tell me it was a heart attack?"

Her face glows to a fire red. No doubt she's embarrassed by all her lying. Maybe I shouldn't push her with more questions. I've asked enough for one day.

She replies, "Remember, I never said the words 'heart attack.' I said his heart stopped, and that was true, just not the whole truth."

All her words sound moist as if she is fishing them out of a lake.

"His heart stopped because he took too many pills. You assumed it was a heart attack, and I didn't correct you. It was a lie, mixed in with the truth."

"Did he take all those pills by accident or on purpose?"

"The doctor's opinion is that it was likely on purpose, but we can't be certain Dad meant for the suicide to happen."

"Did it hurt him? All those pills, I mean. Did they give him stomach pains or anything?"

"No. Absolutely not. He fell asleep and never woke up."

I have another even more important question which has been scrolling across my eyeballs on a continuous loop. It makes all the others seem insignificant.

"Why would he leave me, er...I mean us, if he loved us?"

The one part of my life I have no doubt about is that my parents always loved me. This is as constant as the morning sun or the salty taste of the ocean.

"Rocky, he loved you so much, and he was the best father." Mom takes my face between her hands. "He had an illness for a long time that was difficult to control. He wouldn't hurt you ever."

"How could he have problems so bad he wouldn't want to stick around to do stuff with me? He promised to teach me sailing. We were gonna rent a sailboat and head south to Disney World."

Mom flashes the barest hint of a smile even during this sad talking. "He had a lot of interesting ideas, didn't he? I never heard that one before."

"Why were you afraid of telling me the truth?" I ask.

Mom lowers her hands from my face and puts them in her lap. She studies them as if there is some coded message in their veins and lines.

Maybe this is a question I shouldn't be asking. I pull it back. "Never mind, you don't have to answer if you don't want to. I trust you have a good reason." I hope she hears there isn't an ounce of snark in my voice.

"Thank you for trusting me. That's precious to me. I promise to guard your trust as a sacred treasure between us forever. I never want to lose it again. I was concerned that some kids might think that suicide is a solution when things go wrong or get difficult. Whatever problems a kid may have at school or at home, they should know there is help."

"I understand. Mom, I'm not going to fall apart."

She kisses my forehead. "Rocky, things will occur to you, and you'll want answers. If I don't know them, you can ask a mental health professional. The school counselor is excellent, but a psychologist who has experience in these matters might be better. I'll make an appointment for you to meet with someone, and then we'll take it from there. We can also go together sometimes if it would be helpful."

"Are you worried about me?"

"Well, this is difficult to understand."

"I'm really okay. You'll see."

"Give yourself time to absorb everything. Come down to eat when you're ready."

As soon as she leaves, a river of memories floods my mind. Those business trips. Those days Dad was totally exhausted and couldn't do a thing. Those crazy projects which never got finished. I didn't put it all together.

I wonder if the not-a-ghost dad will disappear for good now that I know the truth. I'd miss him hanging around in my head, even though his girl-boy advice is annoying.

As if my thoughts summon him forward, Dad says, I won't ever leave you. I hope you can forgive me. His voice vibrates as if he's caught in an earthquake.

I bet he thinks I'm super mad at him, but I'm not. Being ill is so not his fault.

I have to prove to Dad I'm not angry with him.

CHAPTER 33

As my eyes close, empty pill bottles float into view and fade off into the distance. Then my bike appears. It's in perfect condition going down a super highway without a rider. The scene that follows stars the woman at Kenmore Hospital. She motions with her finger for me to come inside, but I don't go. When that picture leaves, there's Mr. Novick talking to a policeman, and I'm in the squad car in handcuffs.

The visions go blurry until the cement path at my old house comes into focus. Our initials wriggle inside the heart, and then Dad's letters fly away.

The screen in my head goes dark when a knock at the door wakes me. I'm not sure if I was ever really asleep.

"Come in." I give Mom permission to enter.

She says, "It's almost seven. You must be hungry."

When she mentions food, I realize I'm starved. I haven't eaten since the energy bars hours ago.

"Coming right down." My stomach does tumbling acrobatics, joyful to soon be on the receiving end of new supplies. "But I have more questions." I sit up.

Mom and I lock eyes. "I'll answer if I can, or I'll ask a doctor."

"How many pills did Dad take?"

"I don't know. Maybe it's in the records. I can try to find out, if it's important to you."

"Did Dad leave a note for me?"

"No, he didn't write any last letters."

That's a huge relief. Although it'd be good to know what he was thinking, I'd be upset if Mom had withheld something as important as that from me for all this time. If my not-a-ghost dad was supernatural, he could explain things to me, but he never knows more than I do, so there's no sense asking him.

Mom takes my hand and squeezes it. I squeeze back.

"Did Dad do it that weekend because we were away?"

"Probably. He wanted to spare us. He knew Uncle Bob would be there to take care of things." She bites her lip.

"It must've been difficult for Uncle Bob." I was such a baby, not caring for a second what he was going through. I was only interested in me. That's gotta change if I want people to treat me like the almost teenager I am.

Today is like Honesty Day. I decide to spill everything. "The whole camping thing with Uncle Bob was something Olive and I cooked up. I wanted to get him alone and ask about Dad. Olive had a real science assignment, but mine was phony. I was going to do the report for extra credit so it wouldn't have been a total lie, but those darn hornets stung the life out of the whole plan. I never got to ask Uncle Bob one question."

Mom's eyes and mouth stay soft not like when she found out about my driving. She says, "I had no idea how much you were struggling with finding the truth. You stopped asking me what happened with Dad or why we were moving. I wrongly assumed you were satisfied with the explanation."

"Maybe, it's my fault too for not talking to you more," I say, not wanting her to have all the blame.

"I'm the parent, and I shouldn't have closed off the conversation. I shut down our communication. I'm sorry. We always have to be able to discuss whatever you're feeling."

I stand, snatch a hoodie from the floor and put it on.

"Olive was my partner in all this detective work until the bike ride. She was dead set against that, and I was so bummed because it almost ruined our friendship."

Mom says, "It's grand you have such a smart and trusted friend."

"I should call her. I'll come down right after." Olive must think I'm ripping mad that she tattled to Mom.

"Okay." Mom leaves. I'm grateful she understands I need some privacy.

Olive's number rings only once. Her words run out of her mouth as if they're being chased by wild horses.

"Are-you-okay? Did-you-get-hurt?" She speaks at break-neck speed, a giveaway that she's nervous and upset.

"I'm fine."

"Did you solve the mystery?"

"I did. Give you the deets soon. Promise."

"Okay. I understand. I'm glad you got home in one piece. Why did you stop texting me?"

"My phone died."

"I panicked and called your mom. Are you mad at me?"

"No. I'm glad you did. Honest."

"See you in school Monday."

"At our lunch table?" I ask, hoping our friendship is back on track.

"Of course, and Max can sit with us."

"Thanks. Thanks for everything." As long as I'm sitting with Olive, I don't care if other kids are there too.

Before I go downstairs, I head for the bathroom. After I splash my face with cold water, I study myself in the mirror. My eyes are red, white and blue like the flag, but there is no "after-the-truth" look. I'm still the same, even if I don't feel the same.

A large pepperoni pizza sits in the middle of the table. Mom puts a slice on my plate. I sprinkle Parmesan and crushed pepper on it. She opens a root beer for me. I almost faint. Soda is only allowed on special occasions. I guess today qualifies.

"Grandpa, did you know how my dad died?" I ask, biting off a hunk of pizza.

"I knew," he answers, "But your mom asked me not to say anything, and she's the boss."

"Yeah, she was protecting me. Parents do that."

Mom says to Grandpa, "Pop, from now on, no secrets, and Rocky, there'll be no need for any risky detective missions. Right?"

"Mom, people should know Dad was a fantastic father, the best, and that I'm not mad at him at all.

"I want to redo the funeral."

CHAPTER 34

Grandpa lowers a piece of garlic bread mid-bite. Mom also stops eating. They both stare at me. They seem alarmed by what I said.

Grandpa breaks the silence in an oh-so gentle voice. He says, "That's not possible, Rocky. You can't have two funerals for the same person."

"Um. I know we can't have another REAL funeral, but there should be something I can do. Mom asked me to speak at Dad's funeral, and I wasn't ready then, but I am now. Too sad?"

Mom's frozen eyes blink. She reaches out and takes hold of my chin, turning my face until we're practically nose-to-nose. "No, it's not too sad." She gazes into my eyes. "It's sweet. It's loving. We can have a memorial service for Dad."

"Yes, that sounds good."

"When should we do it?" she asks.

I slide my hands onto my lap to hide my crossed fingers under the table. Her answer to my next question is super important, and the wrong one could be a deal-breaker for me.

"Mom, you arranged the first funeral. I'll plan this by myself. Are you okay with that?"

She doesn't hesitate for a second. "You have my full confidence. If you want my help, let me know." With that she picks off a pepperoni slice with her fingers the same way I do and pops it in her mouth. She'd scold me for that. It makes me smile.

Mom says, "You haven't explained how Dad could have advised you to go to Whitman. Was it in a dream?"

"Not exactly. I'm all talked out. Another time." I'm worried she might get hysterical or do a general freak-out when she finds out about my hearing not-a-ghost dad's voice.

BEFORE SCHOOL ON MONDAY, I ask Grandpa if I can have the service in his house on Sunday.

"Yes, and Rocky, this is YOUR house too."

"Thanks. I still miss Whitman, but it's in my rearview mirror. In a way, a 'fresh start' here will be good for me."

I hand Mom a piece of paper. "Mom, will you take care of the food?" She reads my list of what I want her to serve. It is the perfect menu: pizza, mac and cheese, little hot dogs, French fries, chips, three different flavors of soda and all topped off with snickerdoodles and cannoli for dessert.

With a sly grin and an eyebrow raised in mock alarm, she says, "Hmm. No vegetables on your list."

"Nope. This meal has to be the foods I ate before any green things passed into my mouth. Also, starting today, I'm preparing my own lunch. I'm making changes."

On my way to school my nerves are prickly as I rehearse what I'm going to tell Olive and Max. I wonder if they'll be cool when they find out how Dad really died.

Morning classes drag until lunch. I hustle to the cafeteria and go straight to our table. Today, I don't have to stand in the food line; I even brought water with me.

In no time, Olive and Max arrive.

Olive's eyes pop seeing the array of food I have laid out in front of me. I brought a Fluffernutter sandwich, an apple, corn chips, two cheese sticks and a rather large oatmeal raisin cookie.

"That's quite a lot of lunch you've got there," she says.

"I made it myself," I brag, "I wanted to make sure I'd have enough."

"Well, you succeeded, Rocky. Now I deem you Lord of the Lunch." She does a fake knighting of me with a pretend sword.

"Ha." I laugh at my new title.

No one eats. Even Max, who's usually shoveling in his food fast, hasn't put a morsel in his mouth.

I relate most of the details from the moment I rang the buzzer on the Kenmore Hospital door. My story hypnotizes them. When I'm finished talking, I take a bite out of my sandwich to let them know I'm done.

Max follows my lead and dives into what's supposed to pass for a Tucker grilled cheese sandwich. He struggles to control an elastic-string of a melted material that is probably only 50% cheese, if he's lucky. The ingredients in school food are always served with a heaping portion of mystery mixed in. Max succeeds in pinching off the almost mile-long offending piece.

Olive breaks the silence. "OMG, Rocky, what a day you had! Are you okay? How can you be okay?" I'm surprised as a few random tears slide down her cheeks, but she turns away from me quickly and dabs at her eyes with her napkin.

"I'm fine. Really I am," I reassure them.

"I should have offered to bike with you, man," Max says. "You shouldn't have been there alone."

Who knew this former brute could be such a stand-up guy? Olive's right; he does have potential.

"It was better for me to be by myself," I explain. "It was a lot to take in, but things make more sense, especially why Mom moved us from Whitman."

Max says, "You're lucky you know the truth. I wish I knew exactly what my dad did and why he got into so much trouble. Maybe it's my turn to go on a fact-seeking expedition."

"Sign me up to help, Ginormous Maximus," Olive says.

I add, "Sure, I'll help too. Secrets suck you down like a whirlpool of water circling a drain."

"Thanks, guys," he says.

"Do you think kids will avoid me if they find out how my dad died?" I ask.

"I wouldn't," Max states, "and I'll handle anyone who gives you grief."

Olive gets her scold-face on. "No, Max. Never. We're not doing that. Rocky, everyone will be cool. Like Max and me, they all have stuff in their own lives they have to deal with. No one, and no family, escapes. Things happen to everyone."

"Fair warning," I say, "If either of you ever act different around me, there'll be trouble."

"Ya' think so?" Olive unveils a wide grin to accompany her smart-mouth. "Why? 'Cause you're so important, Rocket Man?"

"I'm not spreading my business all over school, but I'm done with secrets. My friends have to know, or they can't be real friends. If other kids find out, so what? It's time for me to crawl out from under this secret."

"How are you planning to tell them?" Max asks as soon as he unglues his mouth from the sticky stuff.

"I'm having a memorial service for my dad. Sort of like a funeral, but this time I'll make a speech."

"Wow. Was that your mom's idea?" Olive asks.

"Nope. All mine. Will you help me invite the Tucker people? I have a list." I pull out another piece of torn-out notebook paper from my jeans. It includes Ms. Malone and Mr. Handler, Marco and some of the others from the soccer team.

"Invite the people for this Sunday, 1:00, at my house." I'm surprised how the words "my house" slip out without catching in my throat. "You guys can ask your parents to come too."

Olive asks, "Can my brother come? He'll be home on Friday for good. I'm majorly psyched. He got his high school diploma at his special school, which I found out is called Kenmore Academy. He may go to college next September for reals."

"That's great. Bring him along. The Kenmore Hospital where my dad was also has a therapeutic school. That might be where they sent your brother."

"Small world," she says.

"Thanks, Olive, for everything," I say.

"Oh, Rocky," she says, swishing her hair around like girls with long hair do in a show-offy way. She flutters her eyes rapidly, "There's no one like me in the whole world."

"Right about that," I agree.

Max looks like he might puke.

CHAPTER 35

All week I work on my speech for Sunday. My waste basket overflows with crumpled papers of discarded drafts. I discover it's not easy to write about your dead father. There's a lot I need to say.

DON'T MAKE IT A SNOOZE FEST, ROCKY, Dad advises after I've discarded my tenth version.

"Do you have any suggestions?" I ask him. It's easy to get stuck on how someone's life ended and lose the story of the real important parts of their life. I don't want that to happen to my dad.

REMEMBER TO TELL EVERYONE YOU'RE MY NUMBER ONE SON, Dad says.

"Are you kidding? That's kind of wussy, Dad."

JUST AN IDEA. AND THANK YOU.

"What are you thanking me for?" I ask.

FOR NOT BEING MAD AT ME, OR THINKING I WAS A BAD FATHER. THANKS FOR NOT FLIPPING OUT ABOUT WHAT I DID.

"You never have to thank me."

Dad's voice is unusually quiet and low. He needs cheering up.

"Hey, Dad, writing a speech is good practice because someday I may be President of the United States and have to make a ton of speeches." I can almost hear him laughing, or maybe it's me who's doing the laughing.

SUNDAY MORNING, my feet vibrate with excitement the second they touch the floor. I open the window. Mild spring air fills the room, a sure sign the weather has turned. Summer will be here soon.

I run downstairs in my pajamas to make a final check. I tape a large reserved sign on Grandpa's red chair in the den, so no one else sits there. Then I move the small tables and chairs against the walls to make plenty of room for the floor-sitters.

The dining room table is already set with paper plates, napkins and fake silverware. If someone dropped by, they might imagine we're preparing for a party, but without balloons or birthday cake.

Mom's in the kitchen, fussing with something. I come up behind her and put my arms around her, saying, "Thank you."

She smiles at me, but offers no return hug because her hands are deep into snickerdoodle batter.

I snatch a few potato chips from a large bowl. "Should I wear the suit you bought me for the funeral?"

"You don't have to be that formal, maybe wear your school dance outfit. You look handsome in that."

"Okay," I say, happy to be rescued from being buttoned up to the neck with a strangulation tie. I head upstairs to shower and dress.

Ten minutes before 1:00, I stand by the door to wait for the first arrivals and ask the empty air, "Are you ready, Dad?"

TOTALLY READY, ROCKY. He sounds excited even though this whole event is because of him dying.

"Who are you talking to, Rocky?" Mom asks, having taken up a position directly behind me.

I can't dodge this anymore. The time has come for the big reveal. "Well, remember I said Dad suggested I go to Whitman. Well...uh... since we moved here, his voice is inside my head talking to me. He comments on whatever I'm doing and gives me advice. Sometimes, he's in my business too much, which bothers the heck out of me. Is that the weirdest thing you ever heard?"

She doesn't cry or breathe fast, but her eyebrows wiggle a little in a questioning dance.

When she speaks, there's no panic in her voice. "Was that scary to hear him?"

"Yup, at first, I was kinda terrified, but I got used to having his voice in my head. And the strange thing is, Dad never had answers for stuff I didn't already know. When he suggested I drive the car to get help for Uncle Bob, I had the same idea the split second he did. When he said I should bike to Whitman, it was like he was reading my mind. I don't understand how that could happen."

"It's normal to hear the people we love speaking to us whether they're alive or not. You're in my head at times too calling 'Mom.' And occasionally, I've carried on a conversation with Dad too, as if he was right here. This is our inner speech which mirrors our own thoughts or what you imagine Dad would say if he were alive."

"Makes sense." I'm relieved that another secret has been sent to the graveyard of revealed secrets. Mom doesn't act as if there's anything wrong with me and isn't rushing me out the door to the nearest counselor's office. There'll be time for more talking later.

The doorbell chimes, and I let in the first guests. It's Olive and her family. Her brother doesn't say anything but sticks out his hand, so I shake it. Olive leads him into the den. Her mother and father hang back to talk to Mom. Then Mr. Handler and Ms. Malone arrive together.

Soon the den is crowded. Grandpa's in his chair, and most of the kids join Olive on the floor, even her brother. Mom's standing next to Uncle Bob. The funeral was hard on him, and now he has to get through this memorial. He must be dreading it, but I'm not going to make it too sad. He should be okay today.

I place myself in the doorway so everyone can see me. Next to where I'm standing is a table with the photo of Dad and me from Mom's bedroom, my first soccer trophy and those spectacular goalie gloves.

I'm surprised at how unnervous I am as I begin.

"Hi." With that word, the buzzing in the room ceases.

"You all know me, but I want to introduce myself again. My real name is Ronald Owen Casson, Junior. I'm a junior because that's my dad's name too. It's a good name, but I probably won't use it much until I'm an adult. So, for now, you should still call me Rocky, which is the nickname my dad gave me. It was the best present ever.

"This is a memorial service for my dad who died a while back. Some of you may not know he died by suicide."

I let those words hang in the air and pause to survey the room. Olive's brother stops playing with his cellphone. Marco's dark curls lift up from his study of a dust ball on the floor. I have his, and everyone's, complete attention.

I continue, "This is a memorial dedicated to the TRUTH. Everything I say will be honest. My dad had to deal with some mental health issues. And even so, he did a great job as a parent, making sure my life was happy and not affected by his struggles. I'm proud of him and how hard he battled against an awful disease. He was the best father. He could come up with the most unusual projects and whacky experiments for us to do together. I learned a lot about stuff, and about me, from him. He was a wonderful guy. Everyone loved him, especially me."

I glance at Mom. Her arm is circling Uncle Bob, who brushes something away from his cheek. She smiles and nods at me, mouthing "You're doing great."

I center myself with a few quick breaths in and out. "I'm also lucky to have a mom who always has my back. If I ever enter a boxing ring like the real Rocky, Mom would be in my corner throwing water on my face, handing me a towel and dispensing great advice about what my next moves should be."

Mom blows me a kiss with her free arm that isn't wrapped around Uncle Bob.

"So, that's all I have to say for now and—"

I stop abruptly because Dad starts to speak in my ear.

ROCKY, YOU FORGOT TO MENTION YOU'RE MY NUMBER ONE SON.

It jolts me to hear Dad during his service. Olive scoots closer to Max and whispers to him. I'm guessing she knows what just happened to me. Max's eyes bounce from side-to-side. I hope he's not planning something weird. He better not jump up and rush me, thinking he has to protect me. Mom looks concerned and takes a small step towards me in case I'm losing it.

Dad warns me, CAREFUL, ROCKY, DON'T SHARE TOO MUCH. PEOPLE MIGHT NOT UNDERSTAND THAT YOU HEAR MY VOICE. SOME THINGS SHOULD BE KEPT PERSONAL, AND THAT'S DIFFERENT THAN TELLING A LIE.

Dad, I've got this. Not to worry.

My next words boom out. "My dad always told me I was his number one son, and he loved me more than the highest mountains and the deepest oceans. He's still with me now." I suck in a deep breath and finish. "And he was my number one father."

There, for the first time ever, I say those words out loud, the words Dad waited to hear from me for a long time. The words that don't seem dumb anymore.

I announce, "I'm done with what I wanted to say. The service part has ended. Time to eat. My mom has made us a feast."

On that signal, the kids dash to the table. Some of the grown-ups come up to me to say they're sorry about my dad. They better not expect me to be writing any thank yous for their sorrys.

Still locked in truth mode, I approach Ms. Malone to make my confession about Olive and me tricking her so I could photograph the papers in my folder.

She isn't surprised by what I said, and says, "I found the old report card with the muddy footprint in my file right after you left, and I knew Olive and you sat together at lunch."

Those facts clearly gave us away.

"Come for a visit soon, and we can review anything that's in your school file." Ms. Malone's voice flows over me like a warm bath. I could listen to her all day long. I'll go see her. We'll talk.

I spy Mr. Novick sitting in a corner alone. Today, there's nothing jolly about this Santa Claus lookalike. "Mr. Novick," I say, "thanks for being a great neighbor."

He pats my hand. "I was distraught with my big mouth. Your mom called and assured me you're okay. It helped a little."

"You made it easier so she didn't have to break it to me."

"That's a relief. Rocky, you're a terrific kid. This service is a grand idea." Mr. Novick presses down on the arms of the chair and rises to a standing position. "Will you come visit me sometimes?" he asks.

"Sure. I promise."

He brushes the top of my head. At least today, his hand won't get full of greasy gel. I went completely natural.

Olive sneaks up on me and gives me a hardy smack on the back. "Well done, Bolder Boulder. Get it? A homonym nickname. Boulder for Rock. I'm branching out into new territory."

"Not bad. Um...um..."

"Now what? When you hesitate, there's usually another problem dying to come out of you. Who's blackmailing you this time? Out with it."

Our friendship almost ended once; I don't want to risk that again, but I've got to ask her a tricky question.

"Um...do you want to stay after everyone leaves and watch *The*

Princess Bride with me? We rented it, and Mom bought three kinds of popcorn for us."

A pink color starts in Olive's neck and rises to make her cheeks glow. Funny, I've never seen her get even a drop embarrassed. Now, she's the one who's hesitating.

Finally, she speaks. "So, is this maybe like a date?"

"Maybe." But that's exactly what I think this is. I never had a real date before. This will be my first, and it's a whopping, jumbo major deal.

"Cool," she says. And with that one word, it's decided. Olive and I are having a movie date later. So, I guess she's kinda like my girlfriend.

I hug her without caring who might see and whisper, "My dad thinks you're pretty special."

She smiles, and we head for the dining room. I catch the end of a French fry eating contest between Max and Marco. Both of them cram fistfuls into their mouths as the other kids cheer them on. The grown-ups pretend they don't notice a thing.

Mom pulls me off to the side. First, she hugs me. "That was great, Rocky. I'm so proud. Dad would be proud too."

"He told me that already."

"I'm relaunching our 'fresh start,'" she says. "You aren't a child. We have to be a team. To prove things will be different, I persuaded the pro at the soccer clinic to open up another spot." She hands me a black t-shirt with the number thirteen.

"This is the clinic's official jersey. I asked for number thirteen, because you'll be thirteen when the program begins." The back of the shirt has the name Casson above the number.

She continues, "They agreed you could work as a goalie or on offense. It's up to you."

"Thanks, Mom. I play offense for Milton, so I should practice that."

I rush to share the good news with Shawn. "Shawny, I'm going to the clinic."

"Great, you'll stay at my house," he says.

"Okay, if you promise it's not toxic in Whitman. I don't want to stay anywhere that isn't safe. Ha. Ha." Shawn laughs and punches me in the shoulder like always.

I go back into the now empty den for a few minutes of alone time. My eyes pause on the photo of Dad and me.

So, YOU'VE GOT A DATE, Dad says, WAY TO GO, BUDDY, AND NICE HUG FOR OLIVE. THAT'S THE 'ROCKY CHARM' IN ACTION.

Then Dad says, LOVE YOU, using the exact words in the exact tone as he shouted them to Mom and me in the airport security on our way to Florida that weekend.

Those words wrap my heart in a soft, warm blanket.

RESOURCES

Mental Health Resources and Help are available:

National Suicide Prevention Lifeline **1-800-273-8255** is a national network of local crisis centers that provides free and confidential emotional support to people in suicidal crisis or emotional distress 24 hours a day, 7 days a week.

Crisis Text Line is free, 24/7 support for those in crisis. **Text 741741** from anywhere in the US to text with a trained Crisis Counselor.

ACKNOWLEDGMENTS

I enjoy reading about authors' writing journeys. They share genuine stories about how they learned their craft, who helped and supported them along the way, their disappointments and successes. Mostly, they show us their struggle and their commitment to their writing no matter how long it takes them to bring their works to readers.

My journey started at an unlikely age when I was a senior (and I don't mean in high school or college).

I spotted three pennies stacked on a window ledge in my mother's otherwise completely empty apartment as I took my final walk-through. My mind was absorbed in remembrances of her and the void she left in my heart. My mother, Mildred Sharzer, always reminded me to pick up a stray penny, because even that had value.

I pocketed the tiny three-cent pile wondering if there was a message in those pennies that should become a story. To answer that question, I started to take creative writing courses and participate in craft workshops. I never wrote the penny story, but I wrote *Swallowed by a Secret*. My mother was my inspiration, but there are many who have supported my journey. I am in their debt.

My first acknowledgment goes to Staci Olsen, Acquisitions Editor at Immortal Works Press, who "hearted" my Twitter pitch for *Swallowed by a Secret* and put me on the track to publication. I'm overwhelmed that she and others at Immortal Works Press believed my book is worthy to bring out into the world.

A big thank you to chief editor Holli Anderson, who has made the publishing process so smooth for a newbie. My editor, Sarah Hamblin, read the manuscript with careful attention to detail and offered valuable comments which enhanced the text.

One of the best decisions I made was to engage Jessica Bayliss, Ph.D., clinical psychologist and author, to help ensure the mental health issues were presented carefully and sensitively. I'm grateful to Dr. Bayliss for her wisdom and expertise.

Another excellent decision was to join the Inked Voices website that brings together writers in critique groups and offers professional-led workshops. Brooke McIntyre, the founder of Inked Voices, works hard to ensure that everyone in her writing family has the tools they need to progress in their craft.

Through Inked Voices, I had the extraordinary opportunity to work with Jen Malone, an outstanding middle grade and young adult author, whose great talent was matched by her generous guidance and feedback on the first draft of this book.

Special thanks to my friend, lunch pal and former critique partner, Lisa Stringfellow, whose heartfelt writing is as beautiful as she is. Knowing Lisa is a privilege I cherish.

A shout out to my stalwart critique group: Heidi Casper, Kim Holster and Patricia Nesbitt. We have been together for years sharing our work online. They are wonderful partners whose insights and edits always make my writing better. I hope someday we can meet in person, and I can properly thank them.

Dear friends are irreplaceable, and I'm lucky to have Becky Ceperley and Carole Wagner Vallianos, always in my corner. They are the wind at my back. Also, I treasure Linda and Jerry Benezra's encouragement as they followed my writer's journey. My brother and sister-in-law, Leonard and Lois Sharzer, are always a source of constant support.

And for the last mention, I saved the most precious: my beloved children and grandchildren who bring joy beyond measure.

ABOUT THE AUTHOR

Photo by Carter Hasegawa

Born in Boston with the accent to prove it, Risa lived within ten miles of the city for decades until a recent move to the neighboring Ocean State.

For many years, Risa worked in a nonpartisan, not-for-profit organization dedicated to promoting active participation in our democracy with a special focus on voting and elections. Then a strange event that involved three pennies led her to take a deep dive into creative writing, which is now a priority and passion— unless grandchildren are nearby.

At other times, you might find Risa reading, exercising, or doing therapeutic ironing.

This has been an
Immortal Production

CPSIA information can be obtained
at www.ICGtesting.com
Printed in the USA
LVHW091630210820
663838LV00004B/586

9 781734 386615